Pursuit of the Vampire King

THE VAMPIRE KINGS SERIES
BOOK FOUR

RHIANNON FUTCH

ebook ISBN: 978-1-955749-07-7

Print ISBN: 978-1-955749-22-0

Cover by sunsetrosebooks.com

editing by V. Editing Services

Contents

One

Valdís

My eyes pop open and I am wide awake, excitement coursing through my veins like a drug. Squeezing myself out of the cozy nest between Knox and Malic I crawl to the end of the bed and off. What to do first? I need to see Dagma, Kalina, and Katerine. My stomach growls up at me, apparently I also need food. I grab my robe from the back of a chair and slip it on as I walk to the door. Holding my robe closed I open the door enough to stick my head out, "Hi, can one of you go find Dagma, Katerine, and Kalina? Ask them if they would have breakfast with us in the garden? Have food and a table with chairs set up out there?"

The guard on the left smiles at me, "I'll go. Any specifics for breakfast I should let Cook know about?"

"No, I'm sure whatever he makes will be great. Thank you!"

Turning around, I yelp as Knox snatches me up into his arms and nuzzles my neck. It feels really good and has my body waking up to ideas other than what I need to do. Only when he heads for the bed do I come back to the reality that I need to get a handle on my magic before bad things happen. Putting my hands on his shoulders I push and it is completely ineffective. I could push a boulder just as well. "Knox! Knox, I can't right now. I have work to do."

That's when I feel Malic's hands stroking my back and his teeth nipping my shoulder. Knox is kissing his way down the vee of my robe as he says, "Work can wait."

Malic whispers into my ear, "What is it that presses you so this morning my queen?"

A shiver runs through me and formulating words is hard for a moment but I get there, "Magic! My magic. It's not ok, hoooo my, you have to stop Knox, I can't think like this." Knox pulls his lips away from my now very heated skin and some of the blood returns to my brain, "I didn't want you to worry last night but the fact is that I have to get control of my magic really quick or..."

Malic leans around to look me in the eye, "**Or** what?"

"Or bad things will happen. I am kind of a ticking bomb until I get some control of my magic. Without that control it goes crazy and well, it could be very explosive."

Knox stands, "Very well. If you explode, that is not how we want it to happen, it sounds rather permanent and painful. Is there anything we can do to help you?"

Shrugging I tell him, "The best thing I can do right now is to go have breakfast and talk to Dagma before she and I go train. Hekate gave us each our own books. We need to read them and train."

Malic has watched very closely as I spoke. He looks suspicious as he says, "What are you leaving out?"

"Dammit Malic, I didn't want to talk about it." He and Knox cross their arms over their chests, standing there watching me. "Fine. I am the most powerful witch there will be in this time. If I don't get control of my magic it isn't just bad. It is the worst possible thing. Especially since she said I am the key, whatever that means."

Malic sets his hand on my arm, "My queen, you can't keep things like this from us. We are here to protect you and had you not told us this we would have been hindering you instead."

I lean into him, "I know. But I am unused to trusting anyone with all the information. I tend to keep most of it to myself. I need you to be understanding about that until I can get to a point where I trust you enough to just keep you in the loop on all my plans and goings on. You could help with that by remembering that I am an adult and whether or not you agree with something I plan to do, it is still my choice and you don't get to gainsay my choices."

Malic smirks and says, "We are still your kings."

My hands fly to my hips as I lean toward him, "Am I not your queen? The key? And the most powerful witch in all of this world? You keep this attitude up and the first thing I will learn is how to hang a vampire in mid air by his ankles!"

Knox starts laughing as he tugs me toward him and

kisses my forehead, "We will do our best to be less dictatorial with you. Old habits die hard and we haven't had anyone our equal beyond each other in a very long time. Come, let us shower and then we will go have breakfast with your family."

A smile spreads across my face when he says that. "Yes, we'll go have breakfast with my family. I love the sound of that. Malic, are you going to stand over there and turn to stone or get over yourself?"

He frowns at me, "I don't need to get over myself. I," he shoves his hand through his hair and leaving it spiked out at odd angles, "I just worry about you and I need to protect you all."

I take the two steps over to him and wrap my arms around him, "You can protect us without stifling me. I am going to be in danger, there is no way around that. I have been in danger since the day I was born. I need you to have faith in me, to trust that I will do my best to come back to you or to stay alive until you can rescue me."

He sighs as he puts his arms around me, "I will do my best."

"Good," Knox says clapping his hands together, "Now let's get showered before our little time bomb goes off."

Malic and I laugh as we all head for the bathroom, but I can't help thinking I am a danger to them.

It doesn't take us long to get ourselves ready now that they are fully aware of why I need to get on top of my magic.

What they don't know is how terrified I am that I won't be able to, that I will suck at it as much as I have at so many other things. Walking to the gardens we meet up with Dagma and the two K's on our way. We chat about inconsequential things because I don't want to tell them about all this until they have at least had some tea.

Getting seated and tea served takes so little time. Knox and Malic are both watching me so I take a breath and say, "Dagma, what, um, what would you say if I told you that you had magic buried in you?"

She studies my face for a time before asking, "What is going on Valdís? If you need to tell me something, just get on with it."

I nod, "I called our Goddess to me last night. She told me that I am a witch, a direct descendant of her. She said that the shelves where I found the book that told me how to call her to me are filled with the books that will teach me, and you, how to control the magic that is inside each of us."

Dagma presses her lips together briefly and then sips her tea. Straightening she says, "Very well. I know you wouldn't lie to me and you aren't given to hallucinations. The kings here have been waiting for you to make an announcement so they are aware as well. We have shelves in the library?"

I could cry with relief but I manage to control myself, "We do. And one more thing. I have to tell you her name, all of you," I look to the two K's who are completely focused on the conversation for once. "You may have a reaction to it. Are you ready?"

The three of them look at each other and back to me,

nodding. I take a deep breath, hoping this doesn't break anyone, "Hekate."

Dagma puts a hand over her mouth and closes her eyes, a single tear running down each of her cheeks. The two K's gasp, and then the garden freaks out. I can feel the two of them spilling magic all over the place and the entire garden is crowding in on us as I lean forward and say, "Katerine! Kalina! Focus! Deep breath, pull the feeling back inside." They look terrified and I calm my voice, speaking soothingly as I can, "Breathe with me, slowly in and pull all that feeling that is overflowing back into a nice well, yes! A nice deep well. Breathe out and steady yourselves. Breathe in, calming the flow and pulling it in where it can wait in the well for when you need it. There you go, keep at it. You can do it. Very good. Yes, almost there." I exhale my own shaky breath as they get themselves under control. A nervous chuckle escapes me, "I was not prepared enough. I feel like I didn't study for my test and somehow passed anyway." Kalina is the first one to start laughing, Katerine follows and the two of them laughing is contagious. When we have all calmed down I ask Dagma, "Are you all right?"

She nods, "I am. I remember everything she told me in my dreams and it was just a bit to process."

~

Ingemar

My face hurts. Checking the mirror once more, I straighten my jacket and wince as the cut on my shoulder lights up with pain. What was I thinking? Having all of us get drunk and then beat each other up so it looks realistic today? Not my brightest idea. It is done though and we are all quite bruised and battered. Even freshly showered with a just pressed suit I look a bit like a ruffian.

I suppose it will be all that much more convincing. Now, off to pick up that awful woman. Admittedly, if she hasn't gotten herself beat up well enough I would not mind helping her to get to the right look. As I head toward the waiting car Pelos falls in step with me, "Hello Father, you look dreadful."

Refraining from making a face that will hurt I simply tell him, "That was the plan Pelos. We need to look as though the king was violently attacking us without cause. Are you ready to play your part?"

"I am father. Will we be very long? Mother is looking worse by the minute and I want to be there..."

"I hope to be no more than an hour, two at most. If it runs longer I will send you home- you know, I will send you home after an hour whatever is happening, with the excuse that one of us should be with your mother. She is so very ill and the time I had with her this morning was short indeed before I had to ready myself for speaking today."

Pelos nods, his jaw tight. I can imagine the kinds of things going through his mind. As long as he keeps his thoughts to himself they will be tolerated.

The ride to the area in front of the drive up to the castle is short, even with picking up Eirene and Eumeleia. There is quite the crowd waiting as we arrive. The other lords are waiting for our arrival, as they should. I make sure to be courteous and respond to people as I walk toward the podium they have set up for us today. It is no hardship to walk painfully as my ankle was twisted during the brawl. Lord Judda gestures toward the podium as soon as I am on the platform and I go directly there.

"Hello my good Atlanteans! I come to you today with the sad news that our Valdís is still locked away in the castle behind us," I gesture toward it and wince when I feel the cut on my shoulder open a bit. The crowd eats it up. "You may have noticed that my friends and I, along with the good widow Eirene Potentus, are all a bit more worn than the last time you saw us. I am sorry to report that this is because we went to our kings and asked them to release Valdís into the care of her family. King Knox became immediately enraged, attacking the good widow." I hear Eirene start crying behind me and I am impressed, she is quiet but projecting really well. "The other lords and myself protected her and got her out of there at no small cost to ourselves, but this behavior from the king that should be protecting us makes some things very clear. First, the kings are not our protectors any longer, if they ever were. Second, our families are not safe even in our homes. We have not seen our Valdís since she was ripped from my home just days before her wedding should have happened. With kings like this, some mythical enemies from the dawn of time are the least of our worries. It is time for a new leadership. Our small continent deserves better. I ask you to work with us as we try to find a solution, a way to bring about a new way of life for us all."

The crowd cheers for me as I back away from the podium and Lord Judda steps forward to give his speech. Once the eyes are on him I turn around to find my seat only to see my son comforting Eumeleia. How interesting.

Two

Malic

I look away from the conversation as I hear Epaphras nearly running out to us. Excusing myself I step away to meet him a bit away from the table. I know Knox can still hear us but he won't be sharing anything with the ladies still seated around the table with him. Epaphras skids to a stop in front of me, "Sire, your assistance is required. We found them, but they are in bad shape. They can't walk on their own currently and the soldiers were carrying them but there is a crowd and they feel certain that coming up the direct way will cause problems."

"A crowd? Problems? Spit the rest out Epaphras."

He sighs, "There is a rally taking place at the end of the drive to the castle. They are talking about replacing you."

"Replacing us? What? Are they insane?"

"Possibly sire, but that isn't the important thing right now. What we need right now is help getting the two injured people up here through the woods. The guards can carry them but they can't sneak up here while carrying them. You and Knox however, can. And since these are our people we don't want to make war on them."

Knox speaks up from next to me, "We will be right there Epaphras. Of course we will come and get those two up here where they can be treated."

Epaphras turns, taking off back to the castle at a fast clip. Knox puts a hand on my shoulder, "We'll deal with whatever is going on down there later, right now, we need to go get them up here. One of them is Valdís's brother. Whatever you are feeling right now, put it aside while we take care of the ones that need us."

I nod, "Make excuses for us, I need to change out of this. I'll bring you something else to wear. Meet you in the entry."

I hear him saying something to them as I leave but my mind is replaying the last time there was unrest in our country and the words are unclear over the screams and the blood of my memories. I put on the speed and make it to change in moments. A stop in Knox's room and I have clothing for him. By the time he makes it to the entry I am pacing it. The two guards are waiting outside when we step out. We follow them through the woods and we can hear someone giving a speech in the distance. I try not to listen, focusing instead on where I put my feet. All too quickly we come upon them. Our guards are trying to patch them up as best they can but these two, I don't know if they will make it no matter how fast we get them back. The woman, my Goddess, why were they so vicious with her? I look at Knox and he says, "Let's get them back to the castle now."

I walk over to the woman and the guard tending her steps away. I don't know if she is conscious or not but I tell her, "I'm going to pick you up and take you to the castle. I'll be as gentle as I can but it's probably going to hurt some." She moans a little, perhaps trying to agree or tell me no, I can't be sure. I am as gentle as I can be but I can tell I hurt her and I want to tear the people that did this to her into tiny pieces and dance on the remains.

Once I am standing with her I look to Knox and he has Lommán in his arms as well. He looks strained and I know it isn't from the weight of the man. We follow the guards back toward the castle through the woods stepping as carefully as I can so as to keep from jostling the woman in my arms.

Then I hear it. The crowd in the distance is chanting, "Down with the kings." I freeze, a killing rage running through me. It's the same shit they chanted when my brothers were murdered. Knox steps up next to me, "Malic, we have to get them back to the castle. Remember that these people are being manipulated by the outsiders. The two we have in our arms are injured and need us. Finish the mission."

I look toward the sound but nod my understanding and agreement. Knox walks on and I grit my teeth to follow him.

Three

Valdís

The library always feels like home. Most people stay away from books, treating them like they are the bane of civilization. Luckily, Eirene was one of them, as were her lackeys. So the library was a safe haven for me where mostly I was left alone. I trail a finger over some of the books as I remember the many happy hours spent reading while hiding behind the furniture in the library of our home.

The solace those books gave me, I wouldn't trade it for anything. Well, anything other than growing up without someone trying to kill me my whole life.

Dagma is already perusing our shelf when I get there. I hear giggles from a couple rows away and I know the two K's have found their books. I still have the first book with me and I place it back where I found it. It has served its purpose. I don't know what book I should start with though. Studying the titles doesn't help, they all look fascinating. I rest the fingers of one hand on a book at the end

Dagma isn't on and close my eyes whispering, "What book should I start with?" Trailing my fingers along the books till I reach a partition between the shelves I am looking at and the ones Dagma is perusing. Moving down a shelf I repeat the process till I get to the far end. I am back near Dagma on the third shelf down when I feel it, just the tiniest little tingle as my fingers touched a book. I slide my hand back across the spines at a snails pace till I feel that tingle again. Opening my eyes I run my fingers along the spine to the top of the book and gently tug it from it's place.

The book is a good size, not a thick tome but weighty. My book in hand I wander off to find a spot. The chair I sat in before was good but, I want to have Dagma and Katerine and Kalina in with me so I keep walking. Maybe they have rooms in the library? The regular library did. They let people use them for study groups and book meetings and that sort of thing. About halfway down the back wall I see a door. Trying the knob I find it isn't locked so I push it open and find the light switch. The room lights up with soft lights, bright but not glaring. There is a large table with padded chairs surrounding it and I just know this room is meant for me. There is no sign or anything but it feels like mine. I leave the door open behind me as I walk over to a chair facing toward the door and settle in to peruse the book.

Within a few minutes the others have joined me and we are all deep in our chosen books when Epaphras runs in, "We found them! Oh I am too old for this. We found Lommán and Quorin! But they are in terrible shape, I don't know if they will make it."

Dagma and I stand in unison, "Take us to them."

The two older women in our group also stand but it is slower, when we start to jog we quickly realize we are going to leave them behind. Then my two guards step out of the shadows. "Ladies, we could carry you and keep up with them, if that would help?"

Both Katerine and Kalina smile at the offer and I feel certain these men are about to be mildly traumatized. They each pick up one of them and we take off, dashing across the castle to the infirmary where they have them each laid out on their own bed. There is so much blood. My kings are with them, blood all over their fronts and I know they must have brought them here.

Chance

If it was so important for me to get home why didn't anyone meet me at the dock and why in the hell do they have some nasty ass bush surrounding the place? It took me a fucking hour to find the one damn hole. The guards are really slacking here inside the castle, I haven't seen so much as one. Is this why Malic needs us home now? As I come to a crossing of corridors I watch Epaphras run by followed by two women running behind him and two guards carrying two old women. There are women in the castle? Running around like they own the place? Then a scent hits me like a punch to the gut. Oh sweet Goddess, it smells so good. I was smelling little bits of it before, faint traces, nothing more. But this, this I need to find. I need to devour it, make it my own. My feet are guiding me to follow the group that ran by before I consciously decide to do so. I don't care, whatever that scent is coming from, it's with them.

I smell the blood before I get to the room they are in. Strange that I didn't smell it till I got close. The other scent, that one is in this room too. I see my brothers in arms standing near one of the women, the two older ones hovering near the end of a bed with a man in it. One of the women is leaned over talking to him in a low voice, telling him he is going to be ok. I think maybe that she is his mother. The other bed holds a woman. The only ones to have seen me are the guards standing behind Epaphras, one nudges him and he sees me, "Hello King Chance, so good to have you home without the least bit of a warning as to when."

He scowls at me but I don't care, the woman is staring at me and I can't seem to look away from her as I ask, "What is that fucking scent?"

Malic scratches his chest as he and Knox walk over. Knox says, "We need to go talk privately."

Just then the old ones gasp, the woman standing over the man has her hands on his chest and they are glowing. The glow is spreading through his body. The other woman whispers, "Healer, she's a healer," in a voice that sounds like I want to listen to her forever. What the hell is wrong with me?

Malic pushes me toward the door, "Come on brother, we need to tell you some things."

Four

CHANCE

They hustle me away from the action and that delicious scent. Down the hall to a room with some couches where Knox tells me, "The Outsiders have returned. They are trying to take over our big island again."

I stand, "Ah, then I'll just go hunt them down and we'll be done with it."

Knox steps in front of the door, "You can't. There was a rally today and half the island is against us."

Shrugging I respond, "Then thats the half we don't need. Move and I'll go start the removal."

Malic snarls at me, "Sit down and listen Chance." I watch as he scratches his chest some more, what the hell is that about?

Knox sighs, "Things are about to get so much worse. You aren't the only one we called home. Everyone is on their way."

That delicious smell is suddenly stronger and I watch a

woman's hand rest on Knox's arm for a moment before he moves to the side for her. She walks right up to me and I know the scent is her, before I can say anything, before I can grab her up she looks up at me with those brown eyes and she says, "Hekate."

The word echoes in my mind as memories hit me hard and fast. My brothers catch me as my legs give out under the weight of all of them. She says something else and I watch her figure walk out of the room through eyes that won't quite focus. What did she do to me? My brothers toss me on a couch. I hear them seat themselves on their own couches so I settle in to wait for my world to right itself. A few minutes later the world rights itself and I sit up, "Did she do this to you?"

Knox chuckles, "Not immediately. She told me off more than once and tried really hard to stay focused on her mission to help her people. I was not as steadfast. It also wasn't quite so dramatic for us as we were already seated and talking with her. In the queen's suite."

My jaw drops, "How the hell did she get in there? And what were you doing in there with her?"

Malic laughs, "I felt the same way."

Knox says, "I had suspicions that I needed answers to so I figured it couldn't hurt to let her try to open the door. I thought it would remain locked and I would laugh at myself. Enjoy her for a time and be done. Then the door opened for her."

"She can't be. It's a trick. How does she know the name we were made to forget so long ago?"

Malic says, "Your disbelief is tiresome. The Goddess

Hekate sent her to it. Came down and spoke to her in person. Warned her in a dream of the attack that would have killed us without the warning."

Knox looks a bit like he would like to rip my head off as he makes the excuse that he wants to go check on everyone. He leaves the room and Malic looks at me, scratching his chest again. I wonder if something bit him?

"Listen, I don't know how she convinced you all that she is the queen we have been waiting for, but she can't be. And what is that damnable scent?"

Malic chuckles, "That's her. If it's any consolation, you smell equally good to her."

"No, that isn't any consolation. What would be consolation would be letting me out there to hunt the fuckers against us. **That** would be consolation."

"For the love of everything, do not go out there dispensing punishments among our people and for fuck's sake do not under any circumstances kill off Hekate's people for being manipulated. All you will do is piss her off and that is the very last thing we need."

Malic

"Listen, just give it some time. You know we can't make any really big decisions like that until Vincent get's back anyway. Get to know her. You should probably also know that she is a witch, the top in Hekate's hierarchy, apparently descended directly from her. Her magic is new to her, but maybe don't piss her off too much?" My chest is itching like fire but I am trying not to scratch it too much. I've seen Chance looking at me oddly already and I don't feel so great. Maybe I should go lay down? "Can you do that for me? Just chill until Vincent gets here? We won't make any decisions about her till then."

Chance nods, "Fine. I can wait. If we find out she isn't what she seems though, straight to the dungeon with her."

Chuckling I tell him, "Sure. I need to go tend a couple things. I'll see you later, ok?"

"Sure."

He nods and leans back on the couch, closing his eyes. I make my way to my feet and head for my bedroom. My chest itches so bad, I think I need to have a look at it and see what is up with it. I keep scratching as I am walking. Right as I get to the kings wing something on my chest pops. The itch is gone but now my chest is wet, slimy, and sticky. I feel like hell, weak. My door is right there but as I look at it I know going in there will be a death sentence. No one will find me until it is much too late. My shoulder hits the wall and I drag myself along it to Valdís's room. Pushing the door open I stagger toward the welcome relief of a chair, but the floor rushes up at me with a thump that hurts like fire.

~

Eirene

The rally was a huge success and hearing the crowd chanting down with the kings was exhilarating. The ride home with Ingemar couldn't be helped, we need to keep up the facade of unity. Even he was thrilled with the results. Our plans are moving along better than I could have hoped. I would like to remove the makeup I put on this morning but I need it to look exactly the same when I go out later for the tea with the other wives.

Eumeleia brings me a glass of honeyed wine before seating herself in the chair opposite me. She is looking quite flushed from the attentions of Pelos. I don't like it. He is just as awful as his father, possibly worse because he seems to have inherited his mother's idiocy. Eumeleia arranges her skirts for the fifth time since she sat down and I know she is trying to say something. I simply sip my wine with a smile as I wait.

She clears her throat and finally speaks, "Mother, I want to talk to you about something quite important to me."

Sitting up straight I set my glass on the side table, "What would you speak about my darling daughter?"

She swallows, "Pelos. He does not wish to marry Valdís and never has. He said she was never even worthy of providing a distraction for him what with her loose morals."

"As if he has the space to be bothered about what anyone does."

"Mother!"

"Don't you mother me. That boy has more skeletons in his closet than you would know what to do with. There is a reason I chose to allow them to have Valdís, and it isn't because of his stellar morals. You," I point at her, "do not belong with someone like him and there are any number of reasons why. Just the fact of how little you actually know about him for instance. And what will you do when you cannot have his child?"

She looks so confused and I have to remind myself that I kept those stories from her, made sure she didn't know why she had a mark on her ear or why she must cover it every day, keeping it secret from everyone but me. "We are Outsiders. Some of the few of our people left in this place. That is why their Goddess will never speak to us, but our God does. That is why our family does not live as long as Valdís's family would have. That is why you are no more your father's child than Valdís is mine."

"What? What do you mean he isn't my father? Valdís isn't my sister? What are we?" She stands and paces. Turning to look at me she says, "None of this is even ours. That's why he left it to Valdís, isn't it? Because she is the only one in this house of his line? Oh Goddess, Mother, how could you?"

Standing I walk over to Eumeleia and slap her. The sound rings through the room and she brings her hands up to hold her face. "Now you listen and you listen well, your life and mine depend on our heritage remaining a secret. Our very way of life depends on our ability to keep this estate. Everything I have done, I have done for you! That is why I stayed with that fool Conrí all that time. You don't think I loved him? How could I? He was so weak! Always catering to the bloody fools meant to support our way of life, making things easier for them instead of us." Walking back and picking up my glass, I sip my wine and study her. She appears to be shocked still so I walk over and put an arm around her, "My darling daughter, I only want what is best for you. Surely you can see that?"

She puts her hands down at her side, her gaze on the floor, "Yes mother, I do. I was simply shocked is all. May I be excused? I feel I need to lie down for a time."

I hug her and kiss the top of her head, "Yes my darling. Go lay down, I will have your supper brought to you."

Ingemar

Today was the best rally yet. The crowd chanting down with the kings while being no more than a short hike to the castle, perfection. I know they must have heard us down there with their bat like hearing. I almost wish I could have seen their faces. Alas, I am not ready to die and facing them alone to see their faces would be a death sentence if they realized that I was one of the ringleaders of this entire plan to overthrow them.

I was also quite pleased to see my boy Pelos comforting the young Eumeleia. Her mother must have wanted to lose her mind over the whole thing but she managed to keep her cool, maintaining a facade of tears and pain the entire time. A sigh of pleasure escapes me at the thought that our families could be doubly tied in such a way as to make Eirene unnecessary. What a glorious day that could be.

For now, I will settle for today and the promise of a secret meeting with the other lords. Hmm, I suppose I will need to let Pelos live.

Five

KNOX

Some days talking with Chance is completely pointless and today looks to be one of those days. For me anyway. Any time I have stayed to argue with him when he is like this we just end up out on the lawn fighting. Nobody needs that right now.

He'll listen to Malic though; the friendship between them is different than what he and I have. I realize I didn't decide on a place to go, I just left the room. I don't feel like I could do the paperwork justice right now, not after the other events of the day. I head for the infirmary to check on Valdís and the two we rescued today. I see the ones we rescued but Valdís is nowhere to be found. The doctor is in there and I ask him if he happens to know where everyone went.

The doctor looks up, surprised to see me and says,

"What they did for these two is nothing short of miraculous. How did they do it?"

I smile, "It was magic. do you happen to know where they were going when they left here?"

He looks up distractedly, "I think they went outside? Something about practice?" He is studying Lommán and Quorin again before he even finishes speaking.

I decide to head for the gardens. Valdís loves being out there so it would make sense that after everything that would be where she would want to be.

One of the guards is coming from that direction, "Have you seen Valdís?"

He grins, "Yes, she is in the courtyard setting things on fire and putting them out with ice."

"Really?"

He nods, "Yes. It is fantastic to watch."

"Thank you!" My feet are moving a bit faster as I go to the courtyard, I am eager to see this. As I get to the doors I see Valdís and the two old women throwing rocks at the latest ice creation. The joy they have in doing this, I could watch it all day. I think though, today I want to join in.

Pushing through the door I wait until Valdís has thrown her rock before stepping up behind her and wrapping my arms around her waist. As she snuggles into me I ask, "Is this a women only game or can I throw rocks too?"

The two older women look at me before one says, "You know, I bet he could break this thing in one throw."

The other one agrees saying, "Oh yes! We could bust so many more with him helping!"

Valdís turns to me, "I guess you have your answer. Throw the rock big guy."

Releasing her I look around and find a good sized rock. Hefting it to make sure I know the weight, I study the ice. They have been chipping away at the middle. But the base is still mostly intact. Stepping back I aim for somewhere around the middle of the base and let my rock fly. The ice explodes into large chunks that are melting much more quickly.

We get into a rhythm, the two older women growing things into pretty shapes, Valdís setting them on fire and freezing them, then I throw rocks to break them. I think they are trying to see how thick they have to make it before I need to throw a second rock.

Little do they know I have yet to use my full strength on a throw. I realize Dagma is simply sitting and watching us play. I walk over and ask her, "Would you like to throw rocks with me?"

She smiles a little more and says, "No your highness, I am quite exhausted for all the healing today. They," she sighs and her eyes close briefly, "they nearly slipped away. Every time I got one thing stable another thing went crazy. And maybe it is because I don't know enough about healing to do it right, but it took a lot out of me."

"I see. Why not go rest?"

She chuckles, "For the same reason you are out here instead of working. I want to watch her play. She hasn't often been happy like this in her life. Now that I don't have to hide the fact that she is mine, it's just nice to watch her be happy finally."

"Knox! Do we need to break this one ourselves?"

"Excuse me, it would seem I have some ice to break."

She nods as I turn and with a glance at the new creation, let the rock in my hand fly. It hits the ice near the middle but slightly off to the right to take advantage of a flaw.

The two older women have something else growing almost immediately. They create an intricate design of flowing vines, this time without a central support and now I wonder if they are trying to challenge me or Valdís. As soon as the women stop the growth Valdís is setting it aflame. Between one second and the next it goes from an intricate puzzle comprised of green things to a towering ball of flames.

Valdís is turning it into ice from the bottom up when I hear Chance push through the doors. Her eyes close and she inhales deeply. Losing all her focus. the fire continues to rage atop the ice for a few moments longer till she gives herself a shake and quickly turns it all to ice.

The scent of us has such an effect on her until we mate. And she has to go through it every time she meets a new one of us. Along with dealing with all of our issues. I need to find a way to make this up to her.

I realize the atmosphere has changed around me and I tune in just in time to hear Chance say, "If you had any focus at all, nothing would have distracted you. Unfortunately, you obviously cannot be trusted with the defense of anything important."

Valdís' face goes red and a ball of flames appears in her hand. She throws it at his feet, freezing it as it splats.

Chance, ever the brave idiot, never even flinches. Valdís tells the rest of us, "I'm sorry, I can't practice with the temptation to set some vampire on fire so big in my mind right now. I'm going to go have a shower."

She is through the doors and heading for her room before any of us can say anything.

~

Valdís

Damn him! I found a way for most of us to practice and he just had to come ruin it. Bad enough the scent of him made me forget I was casting, but then he had to go and be a jerk about it? Saying I couldn't be trusted, what an asshole!

I get to the kings hall and I smell something weird. My guards are right behind me and I ask, "Do you smell that?"

They sniff the air and one says, "It smells a little like a rotted sore?"

The other asks, "Who would be in the kings hall with a rotted sore?"

"I don't know, but we should find out, they might need help."

They both grab my arms as I start forward, the one on my right saying, "Let us go first. You can shoot them from behind us."

I nod even as I scowl at the whole idea. I only allow it because I don't want them to face any consequences for my defiance. They open each door and have a look in as we progress so slowly down the hall. Finally we get to my door, the smell is so much stronger here. Looking at my door I realize there are weird stains on it, and dark patches that are probably more stains running the length of the hall. A terrible fear strikes me as they open the door and we see Malic laying on my floor, blood and pus all over him.

Pushing through the guards I drop to my knees beside him, "Oh fuck, oh fuck, go get Dagma!" I look up at the guards that aren't moving and I scream, "Go get Dagma! We need the healer! Go! Go! Go!"

My screams seem to wake them and one takes off running down the hall. The other steps over us to check my room as I lean over Malic and put my hands on either side of his face. He sighs and his eyes open just a little, "My princess, my queen. I seem to be rather unwell."

He coughs and winces, his eyes rolling back. "No, Malic, you wake up! You stay with me! Don't you dare fucking leave me here without you!"

His eyes blink and he squints at me, "I don't think I have much choice in the matter."

I get so mad hearing him say that, I lean over so I can look in his eyes as I tell him, "I swear to the Goddess if you try to leave me right now I'm slapping you back in your body! You are going to stay here with me dammit! If I have to cage your soul inside of you, then so be it."

He smiles a little, "You say the sweetest things."

I hear feet pounding up the hall and I look to the door with hope.

∼

Ingemar

The other lords are trickling in one at a time. The discussion is all over how best to take over the rule of our land. Lord Kleitos says, "Why not just keep them locked away in their castle? Leave them there to rot?"

I interject before that idea can take root, "We can't do that because the plant wall around the castle is not under our control. Eirene has control of that and if we depend on that then she has control of us as well, more so than she does now."

Lord Judda nods, "He is correct. That woman has entirely too much power as it is. We cannot afford to give her more. No, it has to be something else. Something that would get the people of our land fully on our side. Right now, if the kings came down and were able to show Valdís in perfect health and give a rebuttal to our accusations, we would be done. And likely spending the rest of our lives in the dungeons below the castle."

Lord Madhava shakes his head, "Assuming we lived that long. My grandfather told tales of the king's appetites, they may suddenly find themselves hungry."

Lord Leifr turns from his contemplation of the fire, "What if we had the people vote? Our slogan could be something about following the will of the people, not some distant deity that could be dead for all we know."

My jaw drops as I stare at Lord Leifr, "That's actually a rather good idea. Did you pull that out of the fire?"

Rolling his eyes he turns back to the fire, "Some of us like to think instead of blathering all the time."

Lord Judda says, "We can always ensure that the vote

goes our way, who will have the power to go against us? We convince the populace they all voted for us, whether or not they all did. After that it will be much easier to march on the kings and convince them that this is the will of the people they are set to protect. The same ones that fear them since they started taking people from their homes. Of course, we may need to make some people disappear."

Lord Leifr chimes in, "And then we conscript sons from everyone across the land. Tell them the kings plan an attack, perhaps that their thirst for women has returned and they sent us a demand for half the women of the land if we want to remain free. Or something like that."

"You continue to astound me Lord Leifr. It's a relatively solid plan, for all that we need to sort details and polish the story. What say you Lord Judda? I believe this might just be our best chance."

He nods, swirling his drink in his glass, "I think with some polish the entire thing could work out to everyone's advantage."

"Then let us adjourn to my private planning room where we will not be interrupted or overheard as we decide upon details."

KNOX

I am still talking with Chance about being less of an asshole when the guard comes running through the doors, "Your highness," he gives us the barest of nods before turning to Dagma, "Valdís, Malic, you are needed healer!"

Dagma jumps to her feet and can't manage more than that. The guard, nearly dancing with impatience, runs over to her, "May I carry you there ma'am?"

She nods and he has her in his arms and is running through the door another guard is holding open for him. I look at Chance and take off following him. I hear Chance offer the two older women a lift and very shortly the sound of giggles following me. I can't imagine what could have happened to Valdís in this small space of time since she left with two guards. She was still in the castle. We get to the hall and I can smell the rot. Where did this come from? We follow the guard into Valdís's room to find Malic on the floor.

Oh sweet Goddess, it came from him. How? We aren't supposed to be able to get sick or be ill. We are all frozen, staring at the two on the floor. Malic covered in blood and pus, Valdís tears running down her face and the same fluids on her hands.

Dagma is set down and moves quickly to kneel on Malic's other side. Valdís says, "We have to help him now! He's slipping away, I can feel it! You have to keep him here with me, please!"

Dagma spreads her hands, "I'm so sorry, I don't have anything left to heal him with."

Valdís grabs her hand, "Yes you do! You have everything I can give you. Heal him!"

Their joined hands begin to glow and Dagma's mouth falls open, Valdís urges her again, "Heal him! Please, he is fading!"

Dagma lays her hand on his chest, focusing for a moment. "Katerine, Kalina, his wound must be cleaned. There is something in there causing the festering."

The two older women kneel down on either side of him but are having problems opening his shirt, Chance moves fast and rips it open for them while I run down the hall for a wound kit. I bring back loads of gauze and the antiseptic produced on our land. The women pour the stuff over his chest and start mopping everything up with the gauze. I look at the guard, "Bring more gauze, as much as you can." He runs out the door and the women keep working. He is quickly back, dumping more on the pile. They get the wound cleaned and start inspecting it. One points, "There it is!" One pulls tweezers out of her pocket and I wonder why she has tweezers on her but it isn't important so I don't ask. Or I thought I didn't, she answers as she tries to pull it out, "I have tweezers because when you are old like me the dicks are always small and hair springs up everywhere. Both require tweezers. Now shush."

They are quickly murmuring, "I can't get it out. It's like every time I touch it the damn thing digs in harder."

Valdís suddenly looks possessed as she says, "Move." The two older women look up at her and pale as they back up. Her eyes are glowing and her hair is flowing like she's submerged in water. The hand that was on Malic's face lifts and moves to take hold of the sliver stuck in Malic, her other hand never stops glowing as she whispers something unintelligible even to my ears for all that it makes my skin try to crawl off my body. Judging by the shivers in the room, I think I am not the only one with that reaction. The piece comes out easily in her hand and one of the older women holds out a container of antiseptic, Valdís drops it in and we all watch as it thrashes while it sinks.

Valdís says, "You will not have another of my warriors." After that pronouncement she blinks a few times and looks around like she isn't quite on the same page as everyone else. The wound on Malic's chest finally begins to close and I breathe a sigh of relief. Dagma says, "It's done. Valdís, let go. It's done!" She has to snatch her hand away from her to stop her giving more to her, but I am distracted by Malic opening his eyes and starting to move.

Chance

Valdís is holding Malic's hand as he starts to wake up. I know she has to be a threat somehow, I just don't understand the angle yet. I'll keep her under observation until I know for sure one way or another. For all I know, she did this to him. She leaves this room and I am her shadow.

Her scent has permeated this room, I can smell it even over the rot from Malic's wound. I want to feast on her and fuck her till I can't see straight. Focus. She is moving away from Malic, getting out of the way as Knox and the guards help him up. They help him to the bed and no one else has noticed that all the blood has drained from her face, leaving her looking a sickly yellow. She starts to sway and it hits me, she is about to pass out. Fuck! Darting over to her I manage to catch her before she hits the floor, I know what is wrong. I watched the healer as she forced her to stop pumping magic into her. Leaning to one side I put my free arm behind her knees and swing her up into my arms. No one even notices as I leave with her.

I am halfway to the kitchen when she starts to wake up. She snuggles in at first but quickly realizes her mistake and stiffens in my arms, her eyes flying open. "Where are you taking me?"

I am more annoyed for liking it when she snuggled into me and my voice comes out harsher than I intended, "To the kitchen. You passed out because you have all the self preservation skills of a dodo bird. So I am taking you to the kitchen to feed you on the assumption that my brothers would like to keep you around. For now."

She chuckles weakly, "Guess it is good you are not so easily won over as that. I still don't understand why you would feed me knowing you don't like me. You could have let me fall and someone would have brought me something eventually. Or I would have woke up eventually and got my own."

I can't help but laugh, "What does liking someone have to do with making sure they get fed? I'll give you shit tomorrow when you can take it."

Valdís

I am silent for a bit after he says that. The usual thing for people that don't like me is continual attacks. Why would he help me for one and for two, give me a pause on the shit until tomorrow when I can take it? He seems to dislike me intensely, why would he help me at all? Can he really care about Knox and Malic so much that he would put aside his own feelings of repulsion to help me for their benefit? Do people do that? Is it just a vampire thing?

Then what Knox said comes back to me. Are they all really supposed to be my mates? If they are, why the hell do they all hate me at first? Are they just that fucking flawed? I need to talk to Knox about this tomorrow. All thoughts flee as I am suddenly moving through the air and am set gently in a chair.

I watch him moving around in the kitchen as he builds a massive plate of food for me. My ass may be big but I have never in my life eaten that amount of food in one sitting. He sets the plate before me, "Eat."

His gruff voice is strangely at odds with how gentle he was with the plate and how carefully he put together all this food. Fuck it, I'll ask him why he doesn't like me. After I have a bite. Once I finish chewing and swallow I ask him, "Why don't you like me anyway?"

He rolls his eyes, "I don't know you well enough to dislike you. I don't trust you. So far the only thing you have done that tips things toward maybe trusting you eventually, one day, is to save Malic. I saw the healer having to break contact to get you to stop feeding her your power. When you stood and dropped a few shades to a sickly yellow, I knew what had happened. Then you swayed and I thought my brothers wouldn't appreciate it if you fell when I could have done something."

Thinking about his answer I have another bite of food. "So you would do this for anyone?"

He makes a face like I am dense, saying, "Yes. I answered a question for you. You answer one for me. Tell me, what is that scent? Are you wearing a perfume or something?"

I laugh, "They didn't tell you?"

He scowls at me, "No they didn't."

I tip my head to one side, he just lied to me. I don't know how I know but I know he lied. "The scent is me. But you carried me all the way here. You must have worked it out at some point during the long walk."

"I thought that might be the case but I wanted confirmation. Do we have a scent to you?"

I chew the last bite I can fit in me as slowly as possible. All while he waits ever so impatiently. When I do swallow I tell him, "Yes. Every one of you has a scent that makes me a little less focused because it smells amazing. Each one of you smells different."

"What do I smell like?"

With a grin I lean toward him, putting my face very close to his neck and inhaling before I sit back, a silky warmth spreading through my core. "You smell like the woods in summer, like the quiet space when the forest knows there is a predator about. You smell of hunter and deep earth."

He scowls, his brows nearly touching his nose where it begins to slope out from his face, "I don't like it. Finish your food."

"No. I'm full."

"You need to eat more than that. Eat."

"You piled it for a damn giant. I can't eat all that." I stand to leave the kitchen and my traitorous body gets dizzy, causing me to narrowly miss hitting the ground because he catches me. Again. His stupid face is smirking at me and I tell him, "Just because I can't eat that mountain of food doesn't mean anything. I ate as much as I could. If you want to help, then help me get to my room so I can rest and check on Malic."

He grits his teeth and says "Fine." Next thing I know

this shady fucker has me in his arms again, striding back toward the kings wing,

"You know I could turn you in a very obedient sheep dog."

He eyes me, "So do it."

My shoulders drop. "Fine, that is one of the things I don't know how to do. But you can bet I am going to figure it out very soon."

Chance is infuriating the entire way back to my room where he sets me down at the door. I realize he is suddenly incredibly uncomfortable and the perverse side of me escapes before I can call it back, "Don't you want to come in? Your brothers are sure to be in here. We could all sit. And... talk." I can't deny his scent makes me want him almost as much as his attitude makes me want to turn him into a sheep dog. His face when I ask though, the hunger written across it as he sways toward me, the pain as he says he has things to do. "Chance, wait. I mean it. You are infuriating but you can come in. Spend time with your brothers and me."

He stopped when I spoke though he didn't turn around. "I must attend to some things. Sleep well princess."

A sigh escapes me and I swear his steps slow for a split second before they speed up. I shake my head gently; what happened to him that he is so scared of the intimacy of everyone enjoying each other's company? Turning the knob and pushing the door open, I see there are still quite a few people in my room. I wonder if he knew that?

Knox comes to my side and puts a supporting arm around me, lifting just enough to take most of the work of walking off me. He murmurs, "Are you ok? I saw Chance carry you out of here. He looked to be in protection mode so I wasn't worried about him, but you gave too much didn't you?"

"I might have overdone it just a bit."

"We'll talk about that later. For now, you are getting in the bed and then I am getting rid of the people."

True to his word, he escorts me to the bed, leaving me with my dignity as he starts telling people that Malic needs some sleep after the healing and admonishing Dagma that she also should get some rest. I watch as she reaches up and pats his cheek saying, "You are a good man," before she catches up to Katerine and Kalina as they walk out the door, closing it behind her.

I sit on the bed a little harder than I intended. Laying back never felt so good. As soon as I pull the blankets over me a hand snakes over under me and snatches me over to lie next to Malic. I simply curl up next to him, my head on that big shoulder, "I was so scared you were leaving us."

Knox is turning out lights as Malic says, "I was more than a little concerned that today was my last while I was laying there on the floor in your empty room. I was not thinking clearly at all."

I feel Knox slip into the bed, his warm body snuggling into mine as he says, "I was scared you were leaving us when you passed out like that. Where did Chance take you? I am guessing he helped, but I am very curious with how he is acting right now."

"Hm, yes, he does seem to dislike me intensely right now, doesn't he? He took me to the kitchen, tried to feed me enough food for ten people and annoyed the hell out of me."

They laugh and Malic says, "He is already under your spell. Just wait, he'll come around and another one of our group can start to heal."

"Heal? I'm no healer."

Knox laughs, "You may not heal with your magic but you are healing us simply by being in our lives. We thought you would never... We had given up hope of you. And the loss of that hope, coupled with Hekate's silence was wrecking us all."

Malic agrees saying, "The murders on top of those things had sped up the breaking so much for us all. It became so much more difficult to be around each other when over half of us were gone."

I am so sad for all they suffered just to wait for my arrival. Would they even think their sacrifices worth it after they really got to know me? "I'm so sorry that you all have lost so much."

Knox hugs me a little tighter, "We are too. But you know, we'll handle all these things and then maybe we'll give over the ruling of the country to a group of people. No lords though, fuck those guys. I don't really know how it should go, but I think maybe we should try it. Then we will be just protectors. What if we put a group of witches in charge? Maybe, since it has been all men running this place for so long, it should be all women."

"I like that idea. It might get rid of some really dumb ideas if the witches were in charge, since it is only women."

Knox hugs me close one more time and slides out of the bed, "I need to go see about some things related to this idea, I will come back to check on you both soon. Make sure you rest."

I chuckle, "Not much worry that I am initiating anything. My eyes have been closed for the past ten minutes."

Malic's arm squeezes me briefly as he says, "I'd like to take the opportunity, but the healing has left me weak and tired. I am going to sleep shortly whether I like it or not."

Knox chuckles as he walks out, "Good. Sleep well you two."

Seven

Valdís

People have been talking to me since I got up this morning. At some point, it just became too much and I slipped away to the kitchen for some food to eat in the garden. Cook was happy to indulge me since my guards were with me even as I slipped away. They really give me so much more space to breathe when I keep them with me and don't try to get rid of them. Cook gives me a tray with enough food for all of us and two other very hungry people.

Thanking him, I take the tray and head for the gardens. So many people ignored the world outside completely. It was one of the best places to hide from Eirene's rage during the late spring, summer, and early fall. I find the table that stays set up out here now and set the tray down. "You guys go ahead and grab what you want. I am going to sit here and eat; there is no reason you should stand guard hungry so I can eat first."

They are thrilled and quickly make some sort of sandwich out of much of what is on the tray before moving a little ways out to give me some much-needed privacy. It's all been so much. Ever since my Dad died everything has just been one thing after another, people everywhere, and crisis after crisis. How did he keep it together?

How am I going to keep it together? I barely have a hold on my magic and I can feel this tugging, this feeling that there is no time to spare. I have to go collect the other witches or their blood may as well be on my hands. How though? How do I get from place to place? How do I find them to know where to go?

Knox's scent interrupts all my deep worries and I turn to see him strolling toward me, "Hello my darling, what are you doing out here all alone?"

Shrugging, I tell him, "Sometimes I can't handle so many people. Growing up I was mostly alone and I grew to love the solitude. Here, there are people around me all the time. I have to get away to find me again."

He smiles, "Or worry about the big things in peace?"

My lips stretch into a wide smile, "Maybe a bit of that too."

"Then I will leave you to your heavy thoughts and your solitude."

"You could stay, I wouldn't feel so crowded by one person."

His grin reveals his joy and I'm glad I asked him to stay.

Even more glad when instead of asking me about my worries he regals me with stories about when he and his brothers were first made kings. "This one time, Aiden and Brison decided to prank Malic. So they waited for him to go to sleep and piped a large quantity of sleeping draught into him by dripping a numbing agent down his throat before shoving a tube down his throat. Once he was quite full of the draught they took off all his clothing and carried him naked up to the top of the community building and left him on the roof, with his ass pointed up at the sun. When he woke up he saw Aiden's entire tribe, it was much bigger than a tribe by then but we still thought of it as a tribe at that time. They had all gathered round the building to watch him snore. Eventually, someone got the bright idea to toss pebbles at him. When he woke up he tried to roll over and stretch."

"Oh no! He wasn't hurt from the fall was he?"

"Ha! No. However, he was damn pissed to find himself with a sunburnt asshole and thorns from the roses he landed in. The older women took him in hand and slathered his ass with a cream for the burn, giving him a cloth to wear for the walk back."

I laugh at the picture of Malic walking back to the castle with a cloth wrapped around his waist.

"When he finally made it back to us they fought in the hole that became the dungeons for two solid days. The best part about that was the way it loosened up all the soil and the digging went so much faster."

"You all built this castle? The whole thing?"

He nods, "We did. All twelve of us."

"How? This place is massive. Even with twelve of you, it is still so much. How long did it take you?"

"It took us a good twenty years or so. Even with twelve of us and so much strength between us. But we got it built eventually. And when we needed something dug out, we just got a hole started and one of us would pick a fight with another, usually by shoving them in the hole."

"Oh! Didn't that mess up anything you had built before?"

He shrugs, "Sometimes. But we blew off steam and that helped us to work together better. We were still so unused to each other back then, everything was so very new. We didn't know each other very well when we fought the monster. All of us just wanted to save our people. We didn't even know why the Outsiders were attacking us. We didn't call them the Outsiders then either."

"Did you ever find out why?"

"No, not really. The few that stayed went into hiding after Hekate marked them."

"Marked them? How?"

"She marked their ears. They all have a symbol of sorts in their ear, on the upper bony part," he gestures toward the area on his own ear.

"Would it look like a square with wavy lines running from one corner to the other?"

He eyes me, "Yes, have you seen one before?"

"I have actually. Funny story, I always wanted one. I thought if I had one she would love me. I saw the one on Eumeleia's ear once. I asked Eirene about it and she said it was the mark that told her Eumeleia was her daughter, and that I was to be hated because I didn't have one and was therefore lesser."

Knox sets his fork down, "Oh love, I'm so sorry."

I shake my head, "Don't, don't worry about it. It was a long time ago and I just put it away. I mean, on the scale of things, this ranks way below how she wanted to kill me."

He reaches over and takes my hand, "None of it should have happened. You should have been loved and protected."

"Maybe. But what's done is done. Besides, now I have Dagma as my mom. That is a whole dream come true. I always wished she could be my mom and now, wish granted. I kind of feel bad for her. How awful must it have been to watch me in continual danger and not be able to do anything about it?"

Eirene

Lord Leifr is slow. His walk, his speech, his thoughts. I would kill him myself if he were not so easily bought and willing to turn on the other lords. His ability to be in on the inner circle surpasses anything even Hulthen could gain access to, so he is necessary no matter how annoying. When he finally strolls in even my Flavi cannot completely mask her irritation as her lips are pressed tightly together even when she offers a drink to the man before exiting the room.

"Lord Leifr, what news have you brought me?"

He smirks, "We have had yet another tiresome meeting. My fellow lords are less than creative with their plotting." He goes on to explain in rigorous detail about their plans and by the end of it I am stunned at the idiocy even while being surprised at the ingenuity of the ideas.

"They really believe not relying on the plant wall will mean I have less control over them? Of course they do. They also believe that I have no idea what goes on in their meetings." I heave a deep sigh, "Fine. What is their timeline again?"

One shoulder lifts slowly, "I don't know. They aren't very time oriented. It's as if they have had other people making things happen for them all their lives. I can send a messenger to you when they are a bit more concrete with their plans. The second half of the meeting was more about drinking and celebrating their brilliance than anything else."

"Very well. Keep me informed as they start to move forward with it."

"I shall, once we have discussed the matter of payment."

"Ever mindful of the important things Lord Leifr. Let me write you a draft."

Once he is out of the house, I call my God.

"What is it you need daughter?"

"It is more I have news and wanted to consult with you before I made any rash moves. These lords, they frustrate me to the point of confusion." He is silent as I tell him what they have planned. "I want to close the gate before they try to storm the castle like the fools they are. They forget they have attacked once with professionals and failed. I can't imagine it will go any better with everyone's idiot sons quivering before them."

"No. The opening will stay open. This is exactly the sort of chaos I want sown. Having the spotlight on them will make it easier for you to act in the shadows. The kings and the lords will be well occupied with all of this meaning you will be able to slip things into the castle that would otherwise be noticed. For instance, you could contaminate the food going into the castle. Speak to the market vendors. Have the lords tell them not to sell to the kings anymore. Once they have done that you go and convince one to sell them a special batch. With this mixed in." A large jar appears on my desk. It is filled with a white powder. "Then with no other food available to them this will weaken them and kill everyone in the castle."

"But, they are vampires. Won't they just start attacking the people if they get too hungry?"

"Exactly. Go. This is my will."

Ingemar is so quick to answer these days. I almost like that he is trying to work behind my back. "Sit. I have a new plan for you."

He grits his teeth as he sits. I barely manage to keep my face set. "What is it you have decided we should do now Eirene?"

I allow a smile to ghost across my lips, "Cut off the food supply. The kings have it much too easy right now. With you turning up the heat by holding your election, the lack of food will be one more element."

He appears to be thinking it over, if the faint scent of smoke in the air is any indication. Finally, he looks at me, "I think this is a good addition to our plans in motion. With this and the vote, the kings will have no choice but to accede."

"Indeed. Have you set a date for the vote?"

"Yes. In two weeks the vote will happen. After that, we will see what we will see."

Eight

Valdís

The room in the back of the library has proven perfect for our studies. We still have to go outside for some of the more aggressive magics. But for the reading and discussion, this works so much better. Now that we have all thoroughly explored our shelves each of us is settled in with a book. I am reading about a traveling spell when Kalina gasps, "Oh my!"

I ask her, "What is it? What did you find?"

She looks at me with a slightly awed look, "I think we can take down the plant wall."

Dagma leans forward, setting her book on the table, "How? Read it aloud so we all know."

She licks her lips and reads, "On the duality of magic. It is known that what one is gifted to do, one is also gifted to undo. For there is nothing in this world that is not dual natured. Light cannot exist without darkness, and so darkness is nothing without light."

Katerine whispers, "We could send it back to seed."

Dagma shakes her head, "No. That isn't the opposite of growth. The opposite is death and decay."

I look to Dagma. She is pale, her hands shaking even as she tries her best to crush her own hands with how tightly she is gripping them. I realize the conclusion she has come to and I reach over, covering her hands with mine, "You don't have to Dagma, Mom. You don't have to use both sides of your power."

She looks at me, her eyes red and tears starting to run down her cheeks, "But what about when I want to? What about when I see Eirene again? Or when one of her people tries to grab you again? I heard the stories of how they keep coming for you. What happens when I want to use that side? Do I become like them?"

I slide my chair closer to hers, "No. You couldn't. Everything you are describing is only likely to happen when you are trying to defend one of us. Even if you were to see Eirene right now, you aren't going to just murder her for being here. She would have to push you hard or try to hurt one of us. You always have a choice. If this worries you, then we just work harder on controlling our emotions. Our magic is heavily tied to our emotions. You are an old hand at this, having worked for my father and Eirene for so long."

She sniffles and a wobbly smile spreads across her face, "You may be right. I definitely wanted to tell them both off so many times and managed to bury it every time behind six gulps of willful silence. If I can do that, surely I can keep from killing anyone."

Katerine sets her book on the table, "Dagma, you

haven't got an evil bone in you. You just be mindful of your power and you will do fine."

"Thanks Mom. You always keep things crystal clear for me."

I can't help but laugh at the wry tone of her voice even as my thoughts stray back to what started all this, "Kalina, do you think you and Katerine could really take down the plant wall?"

Katerine looks directly at me, "I know we can. But should we? Right now they can only come at this place one way."

Nodding, I say, "You're right. We shouldn't touch it for now. But eventually, we may need to be the ones to take it down. To reveal our presence. I think Eirene and Ingemar have convinced over half the continent that the kings are either holding me prisoner in the dungeons or I am dead from blood loss."

Dagma's head suddenly turns sharply toward the door and I pull power, ready to freeze whatever is on the other side when she says, "Chance is spying on you again. He is really determined to catch you at something."

My eyes roll of their own accord as I release the power slowly, "He is convinced I have ulterior motives. It's dumb. He's dumb. I should freeze his head and leave him there till it melts."

Dagma gasps in horror, "Valdís! You better not! He's still one of the kings and you can't go around calling him dumb." She lowers her voice to a whisper, "And he is right outside! He can hear you!"

"Good. And since he is eavesdropping, he will be

hearing your whisper. But better yet, IF I SHOUT, IT HURTS HIS STUPID EARS."

Kalina and Katerine start laughing as I shout, and we hear a low groan outside the door. I can't help but laugh too. Dagma stands and throws the door open, knocking our eavesdropping king over and the three of us are done. I am laughing so hard my sides hurt. Then I realize I am hearing Dagma tell Chance off for spying on me like this and I fall out of my chair.

When the laughter dies I realize Dagma is standing over me, hands on her hips and her brows pulled down. "Oh! Um. Hm. Yes. I suppose I should get up now..."

She grins at me, "Yes, you should. Quit laughing at that poor man, he's got it bad and just hasn't realized it yet. He is off to other places for now but he won't be able to stay away from you for very long."

Chance

Dammit. How did they know I was outside the door? That Dagma has entirely too much courage, coming out there to tell me off like that. How dare she. I should go back and... or maybe I should steer clear of her for a while. It would really piss my brothers off if I make her mad.

I just have to find out what secrets Valdís is keeping. She can't be all that she appears. And nobody smells that good all the time. She has to be adding something to her bath routine. There is something off about her and I will find it.

I think they may all be in on it. I'll need to figure out a way around whatever alerted them.

I still don't know what it was. I am silent. I know I didn't make a sound before Valdís started yelling. My brothers reveal too much to her, how much does she know of our weaknesses? How easy was it for her to twist them around her little finger?

I need to find out more about when she arrived. That she told me the Goddess' name means nothing. And memories are fickle, untrustworthy things. Since I can't watch her right now, I'll just go find out how exactly Malic managed to get so sick and what dear Valdís had to do with it.

Nine

CHANCE

I find Malic leaving the kitchen and shove him against the wall, "Tell me brother, just how did you get so ill?"

Malic's eyes flash right before he shoves me away. "I got poisoned with some weird shit during the attack, I think. There was a surprise attack that got me once in that area." He pauses, rubbing his chest. Then looks at me with a grin, "Aren't you usually spying on Valdís while she studies around this time? What are you doing here?"

A growl escapes me, "I hadn't realized so many were taking notice of my habits. I am obviously rusty and need to improve. Someone set something in the library that alerted them to my presence. That's the only way I can think of that they could have known."

Malic chuckles, "They are all witches. Do you really think they aren't going to notice you creeping about while they study things we aren't supposed to know?"

"Yes! I am the hunter, the assassin. My job is to be

sneaky. To be unseen. Hell, that's what I do when I am in the Outsider's lands. I let them pay me to hunt their own people. I am damn good at my job."

"I know. I keep tabs on all of you. Walk with me." He starts down the hall in the direction he was heading before I stopped him, leaving me no choice but to follow. "Whatever you may think of her, they are witches. At least one is directly descended from Hekate. You have to know they aren't going to be your average marks. You cannot just lurk outside the room they are in and expect they will be ignorant of your presence because you are super sneaky. So, take my advice and really up your game, or quit, before you get turned into something that will be eminently less useful when we defend this castle next."

"When? Have you got wind of another attack on the horizon?"

"No. But I feel it coming. Like a storm in the distance. The pressure is building."

Valdís

Today is the day! Lommán and Quorin are finally doing well enough to have visitors and deal with life. I have been waiting for what seems forever for them to be recovered enough. I want to know if Lommán is going to be good with us being related. Will he be mad that he has a sibling? Happy?

A knock on my door startles me out of my racing thoughts, "Come in!"

Dagma opens the door, "Are you ready?"

"Yes!" I hop up out of the chair and head for the door. We don't make it very far before I can't take the silence any longer. "Do you think he will be happy about it?"

She looks over at me and takes my hand in hers, "He will be thrilled. I promise. Don't you worry another minute about it. I promise, it will all be good."

We stop in front of a door and she asks, "Are you ready?"

"Yes. And no."

"Then let's get it over with," she smiles and opens the door to a room with a couple couches and some chairs, two of which are occupied by Lommán and Quorin.

I can't help myself, I rush over to each one and hug them tightly, telling them how glad I am to finally have them here and safe. Quorin grabs my hand and tells me, "Sit here next to me. I've been all nerves here in the castle. I remember all the rumors about the kings and what with the kidnapping, wait, aren't you a prisoner?"

"No. Not even a little bit. People really think I was kidnapped by the kings?"

"Yes. So many people saw the king go in there and come back out with you, put you on a bike and ride away."

"Too bad those same people weren't around when Ingemar's people kidnapped me out of the courtyard and brought me back to his house unconscious."

Quorin gasps and Dagma interjects, "While I would also like to hear the whole story there, I wanted to get us all together for a couple of reasons. We can catch up later. Ok?" We all nod and she goes on, "First, Lommán, I have kept a secret from the two of you for all of your lives. I have only recently told Valdís as it became important knowledge for her. Now that the secret is out, well, you should know, Valdís is your sister."

His eyes bug and his jaw drops, "What? Really? How? You know what, it doesn't matter. She's been my sister all this time anyway. This just makes it official. Though, I am going to have some questions about what you and Lord Conrí were doing. Holy shit, my sister is a Lady."

I laugh, "I guess I am. I had sort of forgotten that."

He tips his head to one side, "Didn't you inherit it all? Do you think it's because of the mark?"

My eyes widen, "You saw the mark in her ear?"

"Of course. Nobody noticed me when I didn't want them to. But, that also meant I got stuck in some awkward places. I may have seen some things that possibly I shouldn't have seen."

Dagma glares at him, "We are going to talk about this later. For now, the kings have said you are both welcome to remain here under their protection for as long as you like."

Quorin starts crying, I look at Dagma and she mouths "I don't know?"

I put my arm around her and ask gently, "Honey, what's wrong?"

It takes her some time to get calm. Eventually, through sniffles she says, "I thought, I thought I would be back on the streets again. That I would be... Just, not everyone likes people like me. Eirene hated me. She told them, that, no," she sucks air like she is starved for it, "it's just a relief that I can stay. Do the kings know? Do they know about me?"

Malic answers from the doorway, "We do. And you are welcome to stay here under our protection for as long as you like. If you know others in situations similar to yours, they are welcome to seek shelter here as well. We have kept the castle closed for too long and neglected our duties as rulers. I apologize for the harm you came to because of that. Rest assured, that time has come to an end. I came to let you all know that lunch is ready, when you are."

I look back at Quorin as Malic leaves, "They really aren't the terrible people we have been told they are. Terribly lonely and awfully broken, but not terrible. Also, I am so sorry. I never thought things would go like this. It didn't once occur to me that I wouldn't be back with Ingemar backing me against Eirene. He was my father's best friend."

Dagma says, "I thought since she knew I could reveal her secrets, she would ignore the two of you. You would be forgotten. I didn't realize she would hunt that much harder for the two of you."

I look away, "She has always loved to destroy people. I'm sure she couldn't pass up the opportunity. Especially knowing that all of you were special to me."

Quorin leans into my shoulder, "It isn't either of your faults that she is the monster in that house. We all underestimated her I think. Enough of this. I need the restroom and the lunch the king said is ready. I am always starving since the healing. Is that normal Dagma?"

She shrugs, "I would think so, but I can't be sure. I did

force your bodies to heal from injuries that otherwise would have probably killed you. And I made it go a lot faster than it normally could. So, it is possible your bodies are trying to build up the reserves that the healing used up."

I stand and pull Quorin up with me, "Come on, we'll find a bathroom together and give Mom and Lommán some time to catch up before we meet them in the dining room. I have a feeling we'll be using one of the larger ones today."

Quorin

The damn books are back. These same three books have been appearing everywhere. In town before Eirene's people found me. Now, in my room here. Valdís is a witch now, maybe she can tell me what is going on with these books. My decision made, I pick up the books for the first time and immediately drop them on the floor when a jolt of energy runs through me. What the fuck was that? Nothing else happens and I am feeling a little dumb standing here staring at the books I dropped on the floor. It was probably just a weird thing leftover from the healing. I moved wrong.

Yes. That's all it is. Bending down I pick up these completely normal books and leave my bedroom to find Valdís.

The castle is huge. Three guards and two cleaners later I

manage to find my way to the library where they say Valdís is studying with Dagma. "Hello?"

The library feels like it isn't much smaller than the damn castle. Passing through the shelves I come to the back of the library. There is a room to my left, light spilling from the open door. It makes a stark contrast to the darkness of the library, so much so that I almost miss the man crouched down by the wall. "Hey! What are you doing hiding in the dark?"

The man jumps and spins around, "What are you doing here?"

I start to answer but Valdís, Dagma, and two other ladies spill out of the room. Valdís shouts, "Chance! Dammit! What did I tell you? I swear I'm going to have Malic hang you by the feet in the main hall!" My jaw hangs as I realize this is one of the kings she is yelling at.

He spins to face her and yells right back, "I wouldn't be out here if you could be trusted!"

The two old ladies step forward then, "King or not, you are perilously close to getting a sound dressing down young man! Your behavior is poor and you know it is. Now you apologize and go find something better to do with your time."

He opens his mouth to reply but Valdís sees me, "Quorin! Do you-- wait, you have books. Those aren't library books are they?" I shake my head no and she walks past the king to put an arm around me, "Oh, this is fantastic. Come on in, we have so much to talk about." She ushers me into the room they were all in and the two older ladies shut the door behind us.

"Should we be leaving one of the kings out there in the dark?"

Valdís rolls her eyes, "We absolutely should. And at this point, he should just be glad that I haven't started yelling again. Come sit next to me. Have you looked at these books at all?"

"Well, no. I came to you to try to figure out why they keep appearing wherever I am. Do you have an idea?"

She grins at me, "I do. I'm pretty certain you are a witch."

"A witch? I thought... I mean. I just kind of figured that only women that were born that way could be witches."

Valdís's smile falls and her eyes are just so sad as she says, "The Goddess knows you are a woman, and she isn't shitty like Eirene and so many others. Here, set your books on the table, and hold your hand out before you, palm up." I can barely see through the tears in my eyes as I try to blink them away and fail completely. I get the books on the table and my hand in place, she says, "Now close your eyes and focus on a small candle flame in the palm of your hand."

My hand feels warmer and she says, "Open your eyes Quorin, you did it."

My eyes drift open and through unshed tears I can just make out a small flame in the air over my hand. All the unshed tears spill down my cheeks and a sob escapes my throat. Valdís puts her arm around me again and says, "Close your hand to let the fire go." I follow her directions and she wraps her other arm around me, hugging me close and rubbing circles on my back as I cry.

Ten

Epaphras

The daily reports are getting worse. Today is the worst yet. There is a group of lords planning to have an election according to the news today. The lords are all the more influential lords. Who also happen to be connected to the recent attack.

The questioning of the few prisoners we have has not gone especially well. I worry that if they don't soon talk the kings will decide on much more harsh methods of information retrieval.

The man before me finishes his report and waits for my orders. I tell him, "Get back in the field, report back if you hear or see anything else."

He nods and leaves the office. I sit there a moment more before standing and walking down the hall to Malic's office. Knocking once, I wait for his terse, "Enter."

Once inside I sit in the chair before his desk in this ridiculously cramped office, "Sire, I have poor news for you."

"Well, out with it then."

"The lords that were involved in the attack have decided to attack in a different way." His brows raise but he continues to write. "They are holding an election. They have decided that once they win this election and they can bring before the kings what they are calling the true will of the people, you all will step down and give over the kingdom to them. I feel like we should address this before it gets out of hand."

The king carefully sets his pen on the desk, "Perhaps that is what I want. I want things to get out of hand. Perhaps I want to go bathe in the blood of the people that would have us all dead for their own selfish gains!"

He is shouting by the end of his small speech and I can't blame him. "Sire, I can only imagine how you feel. At the same time, I feel certain that our Goddess does not want a large-scale slaughter of her people no matter how stupid a portion of them is currently. Please, do talk it over with your brothers, and maybe Valdís. She may have strong opinions about this. If she is eventually to be your queen, she should be eased into making these sorts of decisions."

He shoves a hand through his hair, "Ugh. Fine. I'll go talk with them. I don't know if this is going to go quite the way you hope though. Chance already wants to go wreak havoc."

We both exit the office and I watch as he strides down the hall toward his brothers.

Knox

Chance and I are discussing his stupid behavior surrounding Valdís when Malic walks in. One look at his face and I know all he has is bad news. Without a word, I get up and make all of us drinks. They don't really have a lot of effect most of the time, but the ritual of it is comforting when we are dealing with things. Malic is seated in the chair next to Chance in front of my desk when I turn to pass out drinks. I set theirs on the far side of my desk before I sit down with mine. "What now Malic?"

He sips his drink before replying, "They have decided to oust us with an election. The same lords that were behind the attack that got me poisoned are holding an illegal election which it would appear they have no intentions of allowing us to participate in, in any way."

Chance says, "It is pretty likely they are going to ensure they win either way. Why don't we just go kill them? If we get rid of all the lords, then we could get rid of the problem. A little more hunting for any remaining outsiders and the whole problem is gone."

I can't help but sigh deeply. Downing my entire drink first, I tell him, "You know that isn't a route we can take. And we know that Hekate is becoming more present again, right as we are facing this mess. She brought back the witches for fuck's sake." I get up and pour myself another drink, "This is not something we can work on right now but I feel like we should start thinking about doing exactly what they want. Step down as kings. Instead of an election, I was thinking we choose a council of the people to take our places. Maybe we shouldn't be the rulers anymore. Goddess knows we are all sick of all the crap involved in running a kingdom, and were annoyed with it even when we first started."

Chance and Malic both seem surprised that I would suggest this, but it is something I have been thinking about for quite a few years. Every time I had to take on the mantle of king in place, take on the duties of ruler. I haven't wanted to say anything because I felt like I would lose my brothers too if we weren't all bound to come back here regularly. Now that it is fairly certain we are all going to be bound to Valdís, it gives me some feeling of security.

Malic takes a deep breath and says, "I really like that idea. We should do more than just think about it. Let's plan for it. Chance here just wants to kill everyone and be done with it. I," he rubs the spot on his chest so recently healed, "well, I am leaning more towards that too ever since the incident. I think we are not the only ones. I mean, Vincent..."

Chance nods, "Vincent would be over the moon to be done with ruling. You know he spends most of his time away in seclusion at a monastery?"

Pacing slowly behind my desk, drink in hand I say, "Yes. I have a fair idea of what all of you do at any given time. Including you, Chance."

He looks distinctly uncomfortable with that line of

discussion and says, "What exactly are we going to do about this election they are hosting?"

Malic shrugs and I pause my pacing, "What if we wait until they hold the election and demand to see the votes??

Malic chuckles, "Like the people will believe us after the lords have spent all this time convincing them that we are evil. I don't know what we should do, but I know that isn't likely to work."

Knox

The knock on the door is angry and the door opens immediately to admit Cook mad as a badger with a stubbed toe. He stops just short of slamming the door and closes it very gently at the last moment. When he turns around his face is dangerously red as he says, "Your highnesses, we have a problem."

Malic stands and goes to him, "If you need to shout and stomp a bit while you tell us we will let it pass this time."

No sooner than the words cross Malic's lips Cook shouts, "Those fuckers said they won't sell to the castle! They've had enough of the kidnapping and the depredations of our ruling elite. Those dumb motherfuckers think that by listening to those idiot lords they are really doing something! Stupid fucking dingleberries on an unwashed ass! And each of them less brains than a fly! How are we going to feed everyone?" His voice cracks on the last, a sob escapes as he says, "My mom kept me fed while I was growing up, I can't let her starve."

I would almost like to go ahead and agree with Chance and Malic. They would starve our own people just to get to us?

Malic tells Cook, "Put together a list of what we need to be able to feed everyone for a few months. We'll see to it that it is brought. And we'll talk to the women about preservation spells. Don't worry about this, your mother will not starve. We've grown quite fond of Kalina too. She is a good person and we wouldn't have the best chef on the continent without her."

Cook sucks in a deep breath, "Thank you. I just, it just makes me so mad that they would do this. It's like they are blinded to everything but hate."

Chance says, "We haven't forgotten. We will continue to protect the people and the land, even in spite of themselves."

Cooks eyes are glistening as he nods, turning to the door. Opening it he says, "I don't care what they say. You lot are better than all of them, even before Valdís came to the castle."

Knox

We all wait in silence as Cook walks away. When he is out of the range of our hearing, Malic turns to me, "How fucking dare these assholes. We should just kill them all, make our lives simple again. We can get food from the outsiders lands until we can grow our own. We don't need them. Fuck, maybe we should just let the outsiders have them. I don't know. Fuck those assholes."

"I agree with you, but that isn't the path we can or should take. In fact, I think we should give them another chance. One more try to do the right thing. In the meantime, we should pull all the guards to this castle and then send half with the women and all persons not ready or willing to fight. Valdís isn't going to like it, but I think we can reason with her if we remind her about how frail Kalina and Katerine are."

Chance starts laughing and I glare at him. He shrugs and says, "Do you honestly think that is going to work?"

"I do. Valdís is very reasonable and also very protective over those she loves."

He laughs again, "Yeah. I don't believe you are really thinking this through. Can I watch while you two morons try to convince her?"

Malic and I say in unison, "Shut up Chance."

Eleven

Valdís

The last thing I remember is snuggling up between Knox and Malic in my bed. This place is not my room and it feels like I am laying on clover instead of cool sheets. The mist is thick here on the ground where I lay, and I don't hear any strange noises so I risk sitting up to look around. My head out of the mist, I see a woman sitting at a table. There is a second chair across from her and she has the same beautiful blue black hair as the last time I saw her. I call out, "They aren't attacking again are they?"

She laughs, "No child, now come sit so we may speak face to face."

I get up and walk over, noticing as I do that I am wearing my robe. I'm not unhappy about that. Sitting down I tell her, "I thought I would see you sooner than this. It seems so long since I last saw you."

"It hasn't been so long as you would think. When Malic

was dying, I came to help him through you. I couldn't let them take another of my warriors."

"I thought it was odd I didn't remember how we got the sliver out! Thank you, I know you have your own reasons for doing that, but I was so terrified I would lose him."

"I know. I wasn't entirely certain that I wasn't too late. But that is not what I have come to see you about tonight. The people of my little continent are being manipulated by the Outsiders and some of their own greedy fools. My warriors feel like they could best protect you by sending you away to another castle. This is dumb and it will fuck up a lot of my plans."

"Should I give them an excuse or a fight? I know which one I prefer."

She smiles at me, "Fight with them, it will be good for them. But, when you get tired of the fight, tell them everyone dies if they send you away to another castle. Largely because you can't take your books, that special space in the library, with you to another castle."

"Is that possible? Could everyone die if they send me away?"

She shrugs, a lifting of one bronze shoulder, "It is possible but at this time not very probable. What is much more likely is that it makes everything take twice as long. It's annoying and will definitely piss me off. Remind them that I am not the nicest Goddess when I am angry."

"I will do that if it seems necessary to convince them."

She stands, "I must go, I have some other things that must be tended." I stand, ready to leave though I haven't the slightest idea how to do so when she says, "One other thing. It is time. You must start seeking the other witches. You will find the spells you need in a green book titled Traveling."

She walks around the table and hugs me, then looks me in the eye with her hands on my shoulders as she says, "Make sure no one else gets caught. It all falls apart if anyone else gets caught."

Her eyes glisten with what looks like unshed tears right before she disappears. Everything about those last two sentences gives me chills and when I open my eyes in my room, I am shivering in my warm bed between two kings.

Chance

For all that the people of the island are supposed to be trying to get rid of us, there sure are a lot of them still coming here for help. The throne room must have held a good ten supplicants this morning alone. Now that I am finally out of there, I can go find Valdís, see what trouble she is getting into now. No sooner than I think her name, the scent of her hits me. She is walking past me, a crossing of halls. Next thing I know, I have her pinned against a wall, "Where are your guards? Did you ditch them to go start trouble?"

"Fuck off Chance. I'm not telling you shit until you ask me nicely."

I put a hand around her throat, "I could kill you so easily."

She smiles and I can smell the lust, the need coming from her in waves. I want to take her right here, now. Then she whispers, "Or you could stop being a jerk and we could both be really nice to each other."

"Can't handle the scent of me without losing yourself to lust?"

Her mouth, that lovely mouth of hers, turns down at the corners and she says, "Oh, I can focus. I can focus just fine. But you aren't going to like it, or maybe you will." She brings her hands up, resting them lightly on my waist as she presses her body against mine. She is so soft and warm, I just want to sink into her softness. No! I must fight against her! I squeeze her throat lightly to warn her off but she presses her hips against my groin as she moans softly. Then she smiles up at me, "Looks like I'm not the only one who can't focus here. You're so hard," her hand slides across my body and grips my erection through my pants. My breathing is ragged and I can't think.

I take my arm from her chest where it was pinning her to the wall and grab her hair at the nape of her neck, tipping her head up toward me as my lips crush hers in a punishing kiss. Her mouth opens under my onslaught, she presses against me giving every bit as good as she is getting.

I realize what I am doing and it is like cold water down my back, I pull away, breaking the kiss. We are both left gasping for air. "You cannot be her."

I take off down the hall like my tail is on fire.

Valdís

I am still leaning against the wall where he left me just trying to calm my racing heart and throbbing pussy when I hear Malic and Epaphras. Malic must have scented me, I hear him tell Epaphras that they will finish the conversation later. I could whimper with relief when he stops in front of me. Opening my eyes I watch him as his gaze roams my body. His voice is muted when he says, "Bruised lips, hand print around your throat, breathing is ragged, and you smell like all my dreams. Knox wouldn't leave you hanging in a hallway like this, that leaves only Chance." His voice deepens, "I'll deal with him later. For now, my Queen, can I be of service?"

"I thought you'd never ask. Yes, please." Just like that he scoops me up into his arms and carries me off to his bedroom.

Lommán

The castle is huge and when I first was able to walk around again, I started wandering the castle to rebuild my strength. Then I found the guard training area. I've been here watching every day since. The men that beat me nearly to death shouldn't have been able to do that. I should have been better able to defend myself and Quorin. I'd give near anything to have been able to stop them.

This is the third or fourth day I've been watching them and practicing alone later in the garden. Quorin hasn't noticed, she is spending most of her time with Mom and Valdís now that she knows she is a witch too. I am glad for her; she is so happy and she'll be able to protect herself. I am so deep in my thoughts I didn't notice the captain of the guard until he cleared his throat next to me. "Oh! Hi. Um, I was just watching."

He nods, "It is fine that you observe. My name is Narich, I am captain of the guard. I have seen you here observing much recently."

"Yes. My name is Lommán, I am Dagma's son, Valdís's brother."

Narich looks surprised, "It is good to see you looking so well! I was part of the team that found you both. Are you possibly interested in training with us? For all that you were so badly injured, you were still quite fierce in trying to protect your friend Quorin. We could put that ferocity to good use very soon if things keep going like they are. Good people are hard to find in these troubled times."

I can't believe my luck! "I would love to join in the training. You really would want me to join?"

He turns to face me and places a hand on my shoulder, "We would all be pleased to have someone so loyal and protective at our side. I don't know if you remember that day or not, but as bad off as you were, it took three of us to subdue you enough to get you to hear us tell you that we were there to help from the kings. That is rare in someone untrained. If you truly want to join us, come to the yard here at first light tomorrow morning. We will put you with the beginning ranks and let you work your way up. We operate on a system of training that allows you to move forward based on competency, not time."

I nod, "Yes sir. I will be here at first light. Is it okay if I stay to watch today?"

He smiles, "Yes, that is fine. I think maybe you should skip the practice in the garden later. The guards tell me your form needs work. It will be better if you have skipped a day before you start learning."

"Oh. They saw me?"

He grins, "It's our job to know what goes on in the castle and on the grounds. Don't worry, we didn't tell anyone. They said you aren't doing badly; you are just missing some things that would be learned in the earlier trainings."

"Thank you, I promise I won't let you down."

"We have no worries about that. It was those same guards that suggested we bring you in. You'll do well. Now, I must get back to my job. See you at first light."

Valdís

Once Malic had fucked my head back on straight, I remembered that I was on my way back to the library when Chance pinned me in the hall. Luckily for me, my guards were waiting outside Malic's bedroom when we emerged. They and Malic walked with me back to the library to reduce the possibility that Chance would catch me alone again today so I could finish our studies.

I am telling everyone about my dream when all the kings walk into the library. I can smell them and I shut up quick about my dream, telling my fellow witches that the kings are coming. We are all sitting quietly watching the door when they walk in. Chance won't look at me and that is entertaining but not important right now.

Knox starts things with, "We've had some news from outside the castle and it's going to affect you all."

I hear the two K's giggle behind me as I say, "Oh really? How so?"

Malic's eyes narrow. I wonder if he suspects I am fully aware of what they are about to say. Knox continues, oblivious to the tone of my voice, "We have it from reliable sources that the lords are planning an election and very likely an attack after. They are currently trying to cut off our food supply. We can bring in more food, but we were wondering if you knew any spells that would preserve the food we can get here? And beyond that," he takes a deep breath, "we thought maybe we should send everyone that isn't fight trained to one of the other castles where they would be out of the direct line of fire."

I look at Dagma, Kalina, Katerine, and Quorin; each gives a slight shake of her head to indicate they are not going anywhere. I turn back to the kings and Malic is rubbing his forehead with one hand while Chance grins like a fool. Knox is grim as he watches my face. With a sigh, I say, "You had to know this isn't going to be something we will agree to doing. Each of us is capable of doing a great deal in our own way. Between the four of us, we could probably take out an army. You are absolutely not sending us to another castle."

"Dammit Valdís!" Malic shouts, "Why can't you just go along with the damn plan and go be safe? Why do you have to be so bloody terrifying? How am I going to—how are we going to protect you all if you insist on staying in harms way?"

Standing I walk over to take his hands in mine, "I am so sorry that I am going to scare the shit out of you." I bring his hands up and I kiss the knuckles of each. Releasing his hands, I step back, "When you all entered the library, I was telling my fellow witches about the dream I had last night." Knox and Malic groan. Taking a breath I continue on, "Hekate visited me last night. Or rather took me to visit her. The main thing she told me was that you can't send us away. It will make everything take a lot longer and could result in a lot of deaths, including my own. Oh, and she said it would really make her mad and that you should be reminded she is really unpleasant when she is mad."

Knox shakes his head and looks up at the ceiling as though it will provide another answer, "That's just fucking great. So we just have to keep you all here in the place that they continually want to attack. Perfect. Maybe we should just send you all down to the safe room. Lock you up in there. At least then we wouldn't have to worry about you getting kidnapped or killed."

Crossing my arms over my chest, I narrow my eyes at them, "I can assure you that if you try to lock us up anywhere it is going to go poorly for you. I don't care if I have to take this castle apart. Don't you try me on this, Knox. Calling Hekate is a very last resort but I fucking will. That goes for you too, Malic! There will be no more of this bullshit talk. Now, gentle kings, if you don't mind seeing yourselves out, we have work to do."

Chance turns and leaves the room, shoulders shaking with repressed mirth. As he said nothing the entire time I can only guess that he was here solely for the entertainment. Malic is sad but walks up to me and crushes me a little in a quick bear hug. He releases me and his hands move to my shoulders as he kisses my forehead, "Promise me you will try really hard to stay alive?"

Reaching up I caress the side of his face, "Of course. How else could I manage to stick around and annoy you all?"

He chuckles and leaves the room. Knox is still standing there, hands balled into fists, looking like he is about to explode. Moving closer to him I put a hand on his arm, "I know this is coming from a good place but that doesn't mean it will work." He looks down at me, his face set like stone. Reaching up with my other hand, I run it down the side of his face. Knox's eye drift closed and the set of his jaw relaxes just a little. "I need you to have faith in me Knox. And remember that I am no longer defenseless. I love you. Now go do things. Kingly things you should be doing."

He laughs, "Kingly things? What?"

"Yes. You know, all those kingly decisions you lot need to make about things. Shoo!"

He takes my face in his hands, presses a kiss to my forehead and releases me. "You just be careful. I'll see you later."

When the kings have left the library, I close the door to our little room. Taking my seat I say, "Ladies, we are running out of time. There are more witches finding their powers all over the world. Only they are not here where they can find a safe haven. The other thing Hekate told me last night is where to find this book," I tap on the book that has been sitting on the table the entire time the kings were in here, "which has the spells we will need to find them, go to them, and get them back here. The idea now is that we practice these spells and get going fast before they figure out I am leaving them here."

Twelve

Valdís

We have started to train in my bedroom, down in the safe room where there is no way any of the kings could hear us or see what we are doing. I am opening portals, between this room and the one in the library. So far they have worked really well. Today I am going to open one at an isolated part of the beach below the cliff that Eirene had me thrown off, very few people ever go there and it was always peaceful.

After locking my bedroom door, we all go in my closet and I hit the switch to open the door. Once we are in the room I ask, "Are we all ready to try this?"

Dagma is glowing with joy as she says, "Yes! You are doing so well, this is going to go off perfectly, just you wait and see."

The two K's smile indulgently but nod their readiness. Quorin takes a breath and says, "Let's do this."

With everyone in agreement, I bring my hands up and

murmur the words to the spell, focusing on the place I want it to open up and grant us access to visit. A circle of red sparks appears before me, solidifying into a red band around an opening in time and space to the exact part of the beach I pictured! I shout with joy and the others crowd in and hug me saying they knew I could do it. When we all calm down I ask them with a grin, "Want to go dip our toes in the water?"

They are all as excited by this as I am and we step through, each of us in turn. I am last to go and I close the portal when I am through. We spend a happy hour on the isolated stretch of beach, sitting at the water's edge and enjoying the midday sun. Eventually Dagma says, "We should get back. They will lose their minds if they go in your room and don't find us there."

With a sigh I say, "You're right. Let's not scare them just yet."

I get up and the others follow as I move away from the water's edge. Hands up, I whisper the spell and again the circle of red sparks appears. Once it is solid and showing the room we left only an hour ago, we start going through the portal. I take one last look at the water and the sun before I go through. I feel like I won't see this again for a very long time. I turn to go through and Hekate's last words to me ring in my head causing a chill to run down my back as I step through the portal.

Back in the room, we practice the finding spell. With a lot of trial and error, we find out that it works best on a mirror or a bowl of water. It provides an image of where we need to go to find the next witch. With that covered, we go through the book some more and find a language spell. The spell will allow the person it is cast on to understand and speak any language spoken to them. We cast it on each other but find only frustration as there is no way to test it here. Finally, we decide that we will just have to memorize it as well as the other two spells because we don't know how long the language spell lasts. We can't take the book with us so we have to just hope it works.

Chance

They have been in that room all fucking morning. I obviously did not think shit through when I was trying to be closer to the room they were in there in the library. Her guards have been trying all morning not to look sideways at me and I can't blame them. I hear the click of the door unlocking and I dip into Knox's room. I have no desire to be caught waiting for them again and that mouth of Valdís's inspires me to doing things I don't want. The ladies exit her room and start down the hall, her guards following behind. They both turn their heads to look at me as they walk by. Great. Just great. I have to make sure I get in here while they are at breakfast tomorrow. I know she is planning something, I just don't know what.

Eirene

It's been a long time since I went to the market myself

to visit the food vendors. It is open air and the food vendors are off to one side in large tents as their stock varies. Walking through I assess them. Van is too much of a supporter of the lords, he will never listen to a woman, no matter that I am a lady and equivalent to a lord. Willem is wife beater, also not the best choice. Anfield is a cheat, he cannot be trusted. Felix sells only the castoffs he scrounges from other gardens, never having had the land of his own to grow anything. Barry though, Barry is the perfect stooge for my plan. He has been sourcing his food from other farms for years. Robbing the farmers blind even as he charges premium prices for everything he gets from them. Yes, he is perfect for this job and I heard recently that he is ready to retire.

I wander through, making sure to stop and admire everyone's food, even buying some small amounts from everyone except Felix. When I arrive at Barry's tent he is seated in the back, one of his hired helpers circulating through the tent to ensure everyone finds what they need and pays for it. I wave him away as I slowly make my way toward Barry. Stopping in front of him I ask, "How's business these days Barry?"

He peers at me for a moment before he places me and says, "Ah, Widow Potentus, I was sorry to hear about your husband's... untimely passing. And the kidnapping of your eldest daughter. What can I help you with today?"

I look around, "Do you have somewhere private we can speak?"

He looks surprised but nods, "Yes. This way please." He heaves his bulk up and leads me through a curtain to a back room of sorts. He has a desk and a few chairs, waving me to one he seats himself behind his desk. "I presume you have some business you would like to discuss that shouldn't be overheard?"

Nodding I tell him, "You presume correctly. Have the lords come through and spoken to everyone about not selling to the kings already?"

"They have. They were most persuasive and everyone agreed."

"Good. How would you like to make some extra while ensuring that the kings aren't around to buy anymore?"

His beady eyes glitter, "Go on, I'm listening."

"If the kings were to buy tainted goods from the only vendor that would sell to them, a vendor who then retired that very evening, well that would solve a great many of the problems our people are facing. Along with making that vendor quite well off for his retirement."

He smiles, "It sounds like that vendor would need to be well off to cover his tracks as he left town and made scarce for the rest of his life."

"Indeed he would. Which is why it is best for it to be someone who has already acquired a seaside estate on the far side of the continent and is less than six months from retiring anyway. This vendor would not only receive a hefty sum for the job, they would be able to sell off the rest of their goods to grateful castle staff who would likely also tip him very well and never haggle the price."

He nods, rubbing his chin with one hand. "What is it to be tainted with? Will they be able to tell by looking at it or a casual sniff?"

"A tasteless, odorless, compound. One that can be mixed with water to coat vegetables and the like. Anyone doing said coating should wear gloves, it seeps into the skin over a period of time."

"So if I wanted to be rid of a worker that was no longer needed I could have said worker rinse the produce and he would pass at home?"

"Depending on how much he got on him before he finished the task. If it is simple splashing, then yes. If he were to immerse his hands over and over, he's dying in your stall."

He nods, "Good to know, good to know. And what is the payment offered for such a service?"

I pull a folded piece of paper from my purse and set it on his desk. He picks it up and unfolds it, eyes skeptical until he reads the large number inside. He looks up from the paper, "We can do business."

I nod, "Stop at the back of my home on your way by tonight. I will leave the money in a barrel next to the barn. It will be the only barrel there, the lid will not be sealed so that you may check it before you leave." I pull the jar of powder from my purse, "Here is all you will need. Four spoons full in a barrel of flour will fully contaminate it, a half spoon per gallon of water." I set the jar on his desk and stand.

Eyeing the jar he says, "How do I know you'll pay up?"

I look down at him, "I have as much to lose as you should you decide to report me for double crossing you. Your payment will be there. I have no desire to end my life in the dungeons with or without you for company."

He chuckles, "Fair enough. Good doing business with you Widow Potentus, I bid you a good evening."

"I bid you a good evening. You will tell the other vendors something so they don't try to murder you after the king's people leave?"

"Of course. I need no problems as I leave town. You expect the king's people to be here tonight?"

"I do. You should get your employee started on the additives, with or without gloves, as you please."

"Very well."

Cook

I hate that I have to bring guards with me just to go to the damn market. Mostly the vendors in the general market areas don't take any notice of me. That changes immediately when I get to the food section. Van sneers at me before very purposefully closing the front door of his tent. I walk over to him anyway, "Van, please think again about selling to me. I beg of you, don't do this."

He looks at the guards with me, "Get away from my stall you crown sympathizer. I don't want to be seen with you."

"As you will then." I go to each stall and even Felix won't sell to me. Not only that, he tries to attack me. Would have but for the guards. I hear the other vendors laughing. One vendor left before I have to go tell the kings what these people decided. I take a deep breath and head for Barry's tent.

Walking in I see Barry off to the left checking his products, "Hi Barry. Any chance you'll sell to me?"

He turns to see me and smiles real big, "You know, I thought about it and I just can't deny food to anyone. I'm probably going to catch some flack from the other vendors but I'm going to sell to you anyway."

I turn to one of the guards and he nods, leaving to get the large vehicle we brought so it can be loaded quickly. "Wonderful. How much for all of it?"

His brows shoot up and he says, "Everything? Well, let me go do some figuring. Excuse me for a moment."

I watch as he picks up a jar and heads toward his makeshift counter in the back. By the time the guard has parked the vehicle out front, he is walking back to me. Barry hands over an invoice and I read it over. This should last us a few months as long as the witches have the preservation figured out. The price is exorbitant but he is the only one selling to us and is likely to face backlash for it so I pay it and a generous tip. He grins, "Thank you for your business. My man can help you get everything loaded. He is washing and crating the vegetables now."

In no time we have it all loaded and head for the castle. As soon as we arrive, I tell the guards to have my people come get the supplies while I seek out Epaphras. I find him deep in conversation with another guard, he stops the conversation as soon as he spots me and sends the man on his way. "Cook, tell me you have good news."

"I do. I found one vendor willing to sell to us and I bought him out. Did the witches figure out a preservation spell?"

He chuckles, "Yes. Your mother and her sister Katerine came marching into the kitchen earlier and cleared everyone out of the pantry. They said they didn't want anyone in there in case it exploded instead of preserved the food. Whatever they did it dropped the temperature in the pantry quite a bit and it... feels different in there now. So I think it will do the trick. They said it should also work on what is in the coolers and the freezers, even if we somehow lost power."

"Good. Ok, I just wanted to check in with you. I am heading for the kitchen now. We have a dinner to prepare and supplies to put away."

Thirteen

Cook

My kitchen is back to normal for now. For at least the next few months. Maybe this will all be settled by then. Our supplies were dangerously low with all the guards we have here now. Standing at the cutting counter I chop a pile of vegetables while my kitchen moves around me. The sounds are comforting until I hear someone hit the floor. I drop the knife and spin around to see one of my assistants on the floor, unconscious. Running over I get down on the floor and try to rouse him, nothing. I check for breathing and he doesn't seem to be breathing at all. I ask, "Did anyone see what happened? Did he choke?"

One of the other assistants says, "I saw him taste a sauce right before he fell. But he didn't choke at all."

The memory of the attack and how they tried to poison our food hits me hard and suddenly I know what happened. "Everyone get away from the food! Turn every-thing off, wash your hands and touch nothing! Anyone that hasn't touched the food go get Epaphras, guards, and Dagma! Get her here as quick as possible."

Malic

Epaphras bursts into my office like his tail is on fire, "Sire, the kitchen! There's been a death." No sooner than the words leave his lips he is off, running for the kitchen. I beat him there easily, stopping just before the door to walk in. I find that the kitchen is in complete disarray. Cook is crying over a helper lying dead on the floor as the rest of the helpers mill around, staring into space or crying, some pacing with anxious energy. Things are bubbling over on the stoves, I take a moment to turn them off. Epaphras comes in with Dagma. She marches directly over to Cook and the helper on the floor. A hand on Cook's shoulder and she tells him, "I need to check him. If you are touching him, it will muddy things."

He nods and puts his hands over his face as he cries. I walk over and kneel down beside him, putting an arm around him while we wait. Dagma puts her hands on the helper's head and heart, a dim glow spreads over him and her eyes fly open. She snatches her hands away from the helper. "I have to check everyone. This stuff spreads so easy."

I nod and release Cook, she puts her hands on him in the same position. The glow spreads over him and then changes, becoming brighter and almost like fire. Dagma shakes her head, "He is clear. Now. I need the guards that helped carry the food in too." I look to Epaphras and he nods, going to speak with one of the guards at the door.

Dagma moves on to a helper and talks softly to him before checking him as well. I turn to Cook, "Can you stand? Let's get you off the floor." He allows me to help him up and lead him to sit at the island. "Can you tell me what happened?"

Cook takes his hands from his face and he is a wreck. Tears and snot everywhere. I look around and find a towel, but I think twice about touching that. So I fumble around in my pockets till I find a handkerchief and I pass that to him. He mumbles thanks and cleans his face a bit before taking a deep breath. "I was so pleased with myself. I managed to talk one of the vendors into selling us food." The tears start flowing down his face again, "I never thought, it never, I should have known!" He slams his fist down on the counter, "There had to be a reason why any one of them would sell to me this time. He," Cook gestures to the man on the floor, "died because I was too damn stupid to question why the man would sell to us!"

I put my hands on his shoulders and lean down to look him in the eye, "You shouldn't have to think about these things. Listen, I want you to put on gloves and long sleeves. Then move every bit of food out of this kitchen into the closet that Epaphras will show you. Once you get the food locked away in there, clean this kitchen from top to bottom. Everything that was being prepared, go ahead and put it in containers. I will have food brought in from the other castles and you will stop long enough to eat. You can save other lives doing this."

Cook firms up a bit and nods. He is still crying, but he has purpose, and he can cry while he works it out. Once Cook is not facing the body of the helper I pick him up and hand him over to a guard, telling him to take him to the exam room we keep reserved for the doctor to see people in. That done I look around for Epaphras and find him speaking to one of the helpers. Walking over there I tell the helper that I need to borrow Epaphras briefly. He just nods numbly and we walk a few feet away.

"I am going to leave you to make sure this is cleaned up. I told Cook you would assign him a lockable closet to store all of the food in. While you are doing that, I am going to take a dozen guards down to the market and close it down permanently. Then, I am going to put an end to this whole election thing. The people need to know that for now, they don't have a choice in rulers and that the Outsiders are back. That this death, the others that will follow, these are their doing."

Epaphras looks very nervous as he says, "My King, I beg of you, do not do this. Not right now. Speak with your brothers first. Do a more thought out announcement. Maybe let them handle this part?"

Rage boils up in me and I do my best to keep my voice low, "What if they had killed her? What then? We can't handle that after having waited for so long. If we are shattered by the loss of her, the entire island will be lost to the Outsiders."

Epaphras looks down, "I know. I know, my King. But you must do this differently for her sake. She would not want this."

I shove a hand back through my hair, "Fine. I will go speak with my brothers on this. Get the other castles to bring all of their food here. And have all personnel come to stay at this castle. Tell them to shut the gates and lock them, enter the lockdown code on the underground garage controls right before they leave. Contact Gage and Vincent. Tell them to bring a lot of food."

He nods, "It will be done."

Fourteen

KNOX

I am in my office, working away at a stack of paperwork when Malic throws the door open. Slamming the door behind himself as he shouts, "They have gone too far!"

I drop my pen and stand, "Malic, won't you have a seat and I will get you a drink? Then you can tell me just who has gone too far and how?"

"You can get me that drink but I am not sitting right now. I need to move Knox. I need to go down to the town and destroy the market. Destroy all their plans for an election, farce that it is."

The market? Oh no, "Malic, what did they do?" Please tell me she is safe...

"What did they do? First, they refuse to sell to us. So we give them one more chance to do right. Cook goes to the market today and," the dread in me grows and I feel my hands curling into fists, crunching important papers in them, "then one vendor sells to him. He buys it and comes

96

back happy. Until one of his helpers dies for tasting the damn food! They poisoned it! Those motherfuckers poisoned that goddamned food! What if it had been her Knox? What then? I can't handle that, and I don't think you can either. If we crack, the island will fall."

Chance walks in then, "Hey, Epaphras sent me to find you. Said I should be part of the conversation?"

I work at opening my hands as I tell him, "Yes. Sit. I'll get us something to drink. Malic, sit. Pacing won't help." I leave the crumpled papers on my desk as I go to the liquor cabinet and pull out some of the old Scottish whisky I keep in here for emergencies. Making the drinks calms me a little, downing one myself before refilling it and making the other two does more. Drinks in hand, I walk around the desk to give them theirs and finish the circle to seat myself in my chair.

"Now that we are all a little calmer--"

Chance cuts me off, "I'm fine. I would like to know what is going on."

I glare at him, "Then stop interrupting. The vendors got together and collectively decided not to sell to us. We try to let them do the right thing and they sell us poisoned food, First, do we have a plan for feeding the people that are here?"

Malic nods, "We are centralizing the food and the people. All the other castles are going into lockdown mode, no one in and no one out once our people leave via the tunnels. Epaphras will contact Gage and Vincent, they are working on finishing some things so they too can join us. He will have them bring food to replenish our stores."

"Very good. What shall we do about the vendors?"

Chance says, "I vote we kill them all, one at a time. Leave their bodies laying in the market. It will send a message."

Malic nods, "I agree. Let's send a message."

Fuck me. Not both of them with the lust for blood. Not when I want to agree, "I think maybe that isn't the message we want to send just yet. For the moment, Malic, take some guards down and close the food vendors section of the market. It's fine if you take down the tents with some... vigor. If you find the one that sold Cook the tainted food, arrest him and bring him back to the castle, We want to get information from him. Unlike the fucking fools currently in the dungeon, they will not be trained and much more likely to talk about whose idea this was. Do you think you can stick to that plan Malic? We can send guards instead."

Malic grumbles, "I don't like it, but yes. I will. I see the wisdom in it even if I would much rather just go about ripping heads off and stuffing them into other orifices."

"Good job. Take some guards with you, and keep your temper under control."

Valdís

I am dreaming again. I have to be because I know I haven't figured out how to float through the air like this. I am in a woman's house; she is waking up because she has set her sheet on fire with her magic. She is frantic as she smothers the flames with her pillow before they can grow larger than a candle flame.

A scream elsewhere in the house, she runs to a different room as her husband sleeps on. I float along after her as she runs into another room. Her daughter has set her bed on fire as well. The mother throws the blanket over the flames, smothering them before they can spread further or injure her daughter.

I am taken to so many homes, women and their daughters waking up to newly emerged powers.

The dream shifts and I watch Hekate telling these women in their dreams, "Go to the castle. Ask to see Valdís, she will help you."

The women ask over and over, "Who is she? Who is this Valdís?"

Hekate's eyes always meet mine when she says, "She is your queen."

My eyes fly open in the darkness of my room. We have to go now or we will never manage to get out there and collect these women.

Malic

I waited till the next day to go into town. After seeing Valdís, she was so heartbroken that someone else had died over this. She still seems to consider the entire thing her fault, no matter that we keep telling her the Outsiders are just utilizing whatever they can to cause strife and had it not been her it would have been something else.

I lay with her and Knox last night, cuddling her between the two of us so she would get a good sleep. She's been restless in her sleep the past few nights. I would swear she is dreaming of Hekate again but she isn't saying. No matter the dark smudges under her eyes telling the truth of the matter,

Today she is with the other witches and they are practicing or studying or something. I have a mission though. Stopping in the kitchen I collect Cook. There are five different head chefs here; there is no reason why he can't leave the kitchen in their hands.

As we walk toward the courtyard I tell him, "We are going to go down to the market and close it. While we are down there you will show me which one of the vendors sold you the tainted food."

Cook eyes me, "What will happen to that vendor?"

Opening a door I stop in the doorway and look him in the eyes, "That vendor will be closed permanently."

It doesn't take long before we are in the food section of the market. People are happily shopping when I exit the vehicle. Projecting my voice I announce, "At least one of the vendors here in the food market is selling tainted food. Yesterday one of the assistant cooks died because of tainted foods purchased from this market yesterday. Until further notice, the food section of the market is closed and I highly advise not eating anything bought yesterday from," I turn to look at Cook and he points at a corner stall and whispers a name, "the corner stall there run by Barry."

One lady comes up from behind our car, she was watching the food vendors with a tear-streaked face when we pulled up. She comes to stand before me, "My son worked for that bastard. He died on his way home from work last night. I've been here all morning waiting for him to get here. He closed his shop. It has sat empty all morning when he would usually be open for hours by now. The lords that say they are taking over didn't give a damn about my dead son. What are you going to do about my dead son?"

I want to hug this woman for her pain but I think she won't appreciate it. "One moment, the other vendors were in on this, I need to send my guards to stop any further sales from happening." She nods, a quick, sharp motion of her head. I turn to my guards, "Go shut it all down. Call me if you need backup." They start for the open vendors, two heading toward each one." I turn back to the woman, "Your son worked for Barry?"

"He did. Until yesterday. He just died as he was walking home. My son was healthy. He was a good man. His girl-friend is heartbroken, they were to be wed within the month."

"I see. We are going to ensure that Barry never opens his stall again right now. But it is very likely that he isn't in town any longer. Do you happen to know anything that would help us find him? Where he would go to hide? Any other properties he might have?"

She nods, "I do. When you find him, then what?"

I shrug, "Then we bring him back to the castle and

throw him in the dungeon. What happens after that is undecided. Do you have suggestions?"

She smiles coldly, "I would love it if you could keep him there rotting and let me visit as much as I like. It would please me greatly to watch his spirit break a little at a time."

"I like it. We can do that. Now, will the loss of your son's income cause you hardship? It sounded as though he shared a living space with you."

She shakes her head no, "He stayed because his father died when he was younger and a lot of idiots came sniffing around back then, hoping to take over the household. He was young, but made sure that they couldn't press too much and ran some of them off when they were ill-behaved. He was a good man, like his father was."

An idea occurs to me and I ask the woman, "What is your name?"

She says, "My name is Karis. Karis Pillais."

"Excellent, Ms. Pillais. I need to go destroy the booth over there. Where should we look for Barry?"

She pulls a notepad and pen from a bag hanging off her shoulder. Writing something on it she then tears the sheet off and holds it out to me, "This is the address to his retirement home. He thinks no one knows about it but it isn't a secret and it is part of the records. I work in the records office. I made note of it when I saw it cross my desk."

I stuff the paper into my pocket. "Excellent. Someone will collect him within the next few days. We would like to pay for your son's internment. It doesn't matter whether you need it or not, it is just something we want to do, if you will allow us."

She nods, "I will. And I appreciate it. May I watch as you destroy the booth?"

"You may. Just keep well back."

She nods and I excuse myself, turning to Cook and waving him on with me. Cook and I go into the tent. For the most part, empty tables litter the inside. I wander to the back and through the flap separating the front from his office. There is a table that appears to have served as a desk and some random papers. The papers are mostly nothing until the bottom two. One is folded and reads the fee followed by a rather large number. The other has doodles all over it. A scrawled note at the bottom reads behind the barn in the barrel. At the top with a lot of flourishes around it is the name Eirene. How coincidental. I slip the two pieces of paper into the inner pocket of my jacket. I leave the office area, studying the roof of the tent and the supports. Cook looks at me, "I haven't seen anything out here that would be useful. Just empty display tables. White stuff on some of them, but that is probably just flour."

"Probably. Or it could be the poison that was used to taint our food. Let me get something to make an envelope with. You didn't touch any of it, did you?"

"No. Honestly, I don't even want to stand in here."

"Fair enough. Where is the powder?" He points off to one side of the tent, "Good. Go wait outside with Ms. Pillais. The two of you should back up a bit further in case any of this gets airborne when I snatch the tent down."

His eyes get round and he beats a hasty retreat from the tent. I collect another paper from the office area and go to the spot that Cook pointed out to me. I see what he was talking about but I doubt Barry allowed anyone to be so careless with his stock. Folding the paper into an envelope I leave the flap open. I run the flap with the grain of the table and manage to scoop some of the powder into it. I am very careful to not touch any of it as I fold the flap in. Shoving it in an outer pocket of my jacket I look around at the interior of the tent one more time. This is one of the most rickety tent setups I have ever seen and I remember back when tents were what we had for shelter.

I walk out of the tent and turn around. Grabbing the cloth from one side of the doorway and walking to grab a section from the other side. Gripping the two pieces firmly I walk back slowly, trying to avoid too much disturbance when it falls. The wood supports creak and give before I have gone ten paces. The cloth falls into a heap and I really think about setting it on fire. But I can't count on even the water men to come to put out the fire right now with the way things are so I leave it. Perhaps I will bring Valdís down one day soon and let her burn the whole food section of the market to the ground.

Fifteen

Valdís

It's time. Everyone is in my room and we have everything sorted. I make portals for each of them leading directly into their rooms. While they collect their packs, I write a note to my kings.

My dearest loves,

I am so sorry to leave without warning like this but I know better than most how much you both would like to have me wrapped in clouds of padding and kept inside the castle for safety. I am going to collect the other witches. They are my witches and I am just as much their queen as I am yours. I cannot leave them to die. Not when I have the power to save them. More will be arriving here at the castle from various places on the island. Please welcome them and keep them safe till I return. And know that I will return. I will always come back to you, even if I have to take the long route.

Yours always,
Valdis

I leave the note on the pillows of my bed and return to stand before the portals as the women return. Quorin is first, she steps through with a brilliant smile. I love seeing her shine like this. Dagma is next, followed by Katerine and Kalina. Each has a bag slung over their shoulder. Waving a hand to close the portals, I walk over to the table I was writing at and grab my bag from the floor next to it. I look around the room as Hekate's words echo in my mind again. I just have to make sure that my friends and the women we find don't get caught and I'll make it back here, one way or another.

Taking a deep breath I sling the bag over my shoulder and bring my hands out to cast the portal to a part of the world I am terrified to visit. We look at each other as the portal opens and I ask, "Ready to go save some witches?"

They nod and Kalina steps up to the portal, "Me first, if

anything is waiting out there you all can save me or close the portal."

I smile, she's so cute. There is no way I would close the portal if something got her. We all watch as she takes a couple tentative steps on the other side of the portal. She turns a full circle and motions for us to come through. I wait as they go through and I finally take my turn. Stepping through the portal I take a couple more steps and look around in amazement. Turning to the portal, I raise my hand to close it when something comes flying through. I know it has to be Chance and I close the portal, "Shit." I look toward the direction he was going and there he is in all his idiocy.

Chance

Under the bed was not my first choice of places to hide but really, this room is poorly decorated in regards to hiding places. Other than the safe room there just isn't much. But I can hear everything from here and I freeze when I realize they are about to leave. They aren't telling anyone and they have a way to go between rooms, between continents, instantaneously. I can't let them go by themselves. My brothers will not survive if they lose her. And maybe I wouldn't be so great either.

I shake my head, that isn't something I want to think about at all. Slowly, I ease to the side of the bed away from the portals I can see the bottom edges of shimmering. Four.

She has four portals going and she is just over there scratching away at the paper, probably writing some damn note for Knox and Malic. I'm going to do them one better. She isn't leaving here without me. The other women return and the four portals disappear. I see a new portal appear and I move to a crouching position while they talk. Peering around the corner of the bed I see one of the old ladies go through the portal. At least they are going to appear in a wooded area. I shudder to think what would happen if they landed in the middle of a city. The women are going through the portal and I creep out a little further, giving myself a better angle to jump through. I know I have to be quick. Valdís steps through and I bolt for the portal. I see her hand start to raise and I fear she will close it so I leap through. Hitting the ground rolling, I stop in a crouch as Valdís says, "Shit," and the portal closes. I grin with my victory until it occurs to me, we are a long damn way from home and I don't exactly have control over the mode of transportation.

She may have been more accurate than I thought when she said shit.

I stand as she stomps over to me, "What are you doing here, Chance? Why were you hiding in my bedroom? Oh my Goddess, tell me you weren't in there last night!"

"What? No. I came in this morning while you were at breakfast. You all stopped using the library and I couldn't keep tabs on you. So I snuck in while you were out and it looks like I was just in time. You need to open that portal and take us all back home!"

She opens her mouth to say something but pauses as we hear a woman crying. "You know what? Come with me,

Chance. Let me show you why we are here." We follow the sound of the woman crying. She is in an old stream bed, a man's lifeless body not far from her. Valdís jumps down into the stream bed, walks up to her and kneels before her, "Are you hurt?"

The woman is terrified as she looks at Valdís, "It just happened." She speaks fast and stumbles over words as she tells her, "I came out here for some quiet and he followed me. He was mad because I won't marry him. He said he would kill me! His hands, his hands around my throat and then, suddenly a light and he flew away from me. And, and..." she dissolves into tears as Valdís wraps her into her arms.

I walk around and jump down into the stream bed next to the man. I see scratches on his face and his body is still warm. I look over to the women, the one that this man followed out here has spots darkening her throat, one of her eyes is swelling shut. Dammit.

"Valdís!" She looks over at me and I hoist the body as I tell her, "Stay there while I take care of this. Don't go anywhere, you understand?"

She nods once, her lips pressed together like she is holding back. Probably curses. Throwing the body over my shoulder I carry him away to find a good spot to bury his stupid ass. Luckily, there is a boulder I can just see through the trees so I point myself at that. The boulder is large but not impossible for me to lift even one armed while I shove a body under it. I ease the boulder down because this isn't my first rodeo and I didn't pack a bag. Walking around with some dickbag's insides stuck to me is not my idea of fun.

The squelching crunch noise has never become terribly pleasant either.

My part in this done I head back to Valdís and the new witch.

Ingemar

This isn't good. The food market closed? If the reports are accurate one of the castle helpers and one of the vendor's helpers both died. And one of the kings went to the market himself and tore down a tent. I pace my office, what am I going to do if this goes poorly? I can't end up in the dungeon. How did they die? Why? They couldn't have starved that quickly and one of them worked for a vendor.

This is not good. Not good at all.

I hear a knock at the door as I am pouring myself a drink, "Enter."

Hulthen opens the door, "Sir, the doctors say your wife is likely to pass within the hour."

I turn to look at him, "Really?"

"Yes sir."

This night may be getting better. "Hulthen, send a message to Lord Judda, tell him I would like to see him and our group. Let me know as soon as they arrive. I am going to see my wife."

"Yes sir."

My wife picked a rather convenient time to pass. She breathed her last, Pelos and I are very sad but stoic. Hulthen arrives to tell me the Lords have arrived and are asking for me not long after she passes. Before I can say anything Pelos says, "Father, you should go. This is important business and I can take care of Mother."

"Pelos, I don't want to put all this on you. It's so much that your mother passed and your betrothed is locked in a castle with those demented kings."

"That is why you must go father. I can take care of Mother's final arrangements. You go and take care of getting my Valdís back."

"You do our line credit. I will leave her in your capable hands. Spare no expense, she deserves the best."

"I agree Father."

Placing a hand on his shoulder, I give it a squeeze before I leave the room. The further I get from that room, the happier I am. She took so long to just damn die already. The only good she did was to die quickly after I arrived at her deathbed. The other Lords are waiting in the study, a fresh bottle of wine already opened and poured for them. "Gentlemen," I say as I enter the room, "it is good to see you. I regret to tell you that my wife has passed just moments ago." There is a chorus of the expected condolences. They appear to mean them as much as I mean it when I say, "She will be missed." A hand over my face for a brief time to seem as though I give a shit. "I have also received news that the market is closed now. That I expected but, it would appear that one of the vendors took it upon himself to do something drastic. A kitchen helper died as well as a vendor's helper."

Lord Judda looks surprised when I mention the deaths and I know he had nothing to do with it. I don't think the vendor did either, not on his own anyway. I notice Lord Klietos looks unsurprised, but that may just be his face. Nonetheless, he bears watching.

It takes half the night and three bottles of my good wine before we decide that the recruiting process must be sped up and the rest of our plans as well. The election must happen for us to continue to have the support of the people as much as we do. Entirely too many people recall that the kings were put in place by the Goddess.

As the lords are leaving Lord Judda stops in front of me, "You are going to go speak to Eirene, correct?"

"Of course. We aren't quite finished with her,"

"Perhaps that is the wild card we should be checking in regard to unsanctioned deaths."

I hadn't considered that and it is a shock to think that a woman would arrange for something like that. But it makes sense. I nod, "I'll see if she will reveal anything by accident."

Valdís

The woman in my arms is shaking still as she says, "Who are you? Oh god, I'm going to prison. They are going to know it was me."

I ease her back with my hands on her shoulders, "You aren't going to prison. We came here to find you. You are one of us. You need training and a safe place to be. We can help you with these things, if you will trust me?"

She lifts her bruised and tear-stained face to look at me, "It's that or go to prison. If I made it there, it's more likely the authorities would have me dead before I arrived. I don't think I really have a choice."

I shrug with a grimace, "You aren't wrong. I promise I will get you to a safe place where these people can't touch you. But first I have to go find some other women like us."

"You said us. You have this power too?"

"I don't know if ours are exactly the same but I have power." I notice Chance standing on the riverbank opposite of where we left everyone else, silently watching. "I think maybe we should get going if that man is going to be missed soon. Can you stand? Do you need help walking?"

She sniffs once more and looks down the river bed. Turning back to me she says, "No, I can get up and I can walk. Let's get out of here before they start the search."

Chance leaps across the river bed and helps her climb out. Once she is on solid ground he reaches down to grab me as I am half up the side, lifting me out and setting me on my feet entirely too close to him, all the air seems to suddenly be gone from this part of the woods. "Um, thanks."

He nods and steps back like he is afraid of being burnt. The air is back and I turn away from him as I work on breathing right again. I take her arm and lead her back toward the others.

Dagma heals the woman while I work the spell to find the next witch. It is weird to do it with Chance watching over my shoulder. I manage it and this place seems like a beach with no sand.

Chance sees the image and snorts, "The desert. Fucking wonderful."

I roll my eyes, "It's not like I choose where. The spell takes me to the one most in need. Maybe you should just get ready for a fight."

"Fucking wonderful." He pulls a device out of his pocket and starts tapping away at it.

"What is that?"

"Phone."

"Why are you tapping it like that?"

"Sending a message to Malic and Knox, who would both probably like to throttle you right about now."

"I suppose they might. Won't they be cheered to know you are here?" He looks up at me puzzled, and I narrow my eyes at him. He snorts and I tell him, "Back up. I need my elbow space to get this spell right."

His lips twist but he takes a single step back. I guess it will have to do. Putting my hands up, I work the spell and hear a gasp from behind me. The woman is staring at the portal, "Oh my god. Can I learn to do that?"

I shrug, "Probably? As long as you have the power to hold it. Time to go ladies, before people come looking for her and the guy that tried her today."

The women all gather their things and start through the portal. The woman is nervous about going through but I don't get the chance to convince her as Quorin walks up beside her and says, "I was scared the first time too. We can go through together."

The woman nods, "I would like that. I'm not usually so scared but--"

Quorin holds up a hand, "It's okay to be scared. What you went through today would be a lot for anyone." She brings that same hand down and holds it out toward the woman. The woman takes Quorin's hand in hers and they walk thru the portal hand in hand.

KNOX

My stomach growls and I realize I have been working on these plans all morning. And I skipped breakfast. I wonder if Valdís has had lunch yet? I get up and head for the library, it is pretty close to my office. No guards at the door, and no one inside. Hm. Maybe they are still working in Valdís's room to avoid Chance's spying.

I get there and find her guards standing outside the room but the room is empty. "Where did she go and why aren't you with her?"

The guards' eyes go round and they say, "Sire, she hasn't left. We walked back here with her and the other women."

"Search the room, I'll check the kitchens." By the time I get to the kitchen, the castle is searching for her.

As I come out and start toward the gardens one of her guards comes running waving a piece of paper, "Sire! She left a note!"

He hands me the paper and Malic arrives at my side as I

open it. Angling it so we can both see it, I start cursing as I realize what she has done. Malic is silent and then his phone beeps. I look around and realize I have yet to see Chance. Chance who was determined to spy on her...

Malic shows me the text:

> Your little lunatic took us to the Outsider's lands. I don't know where we are but we are going to a desert next. She's rescuing witches. They are all insane. I've already buried a man. No, it wasn't my kill. Will message when I can.

"Ah fuck."

~

Eirene

That fool Ingemar is scared shitless about the deaths and the closure of the market. So scared he has shown up unannounced thinking I know nothing.

"Eirene, I don't know how it happened, but two people died and now the kings are coming out of the castle and doing things. The last thing we need is for them to start wandering around talking to people. This election has to go off without a hitch and it needs to at least appear like they knew and did nothing."

Watching him, I realize he suspects I had something to do with the deaths. He isn't wrong but I don't want his thoughts going in that direction. "It's really quite perfect that they have come out and messed things up before retreating back into their castle without talking to anyone."

"But they did talk! The king made a proclamation that the food market is closed."

"Ingemar, how very common of you to be unable to tell the difference between a proclamation and talking to someone. The king didn't stop and talk to any of the people shopping there, just told everyone he was closing it down. Probably didn't even say why. This is going better than we could have hoped. All we have to do now is let them be until you can get your election finished. Hold it early due to the cruel deprivations the kings are inflicting upon the people. You intend that you will win no matter the actual outcome, yes?"

"Of course. We can't leave something so important up to those fool commoners."

"Then go forth and be elected. Keep in mind when you go to the castle, that plant wall is poison to everyone. Flavi!"

She opens the door saying, "Yes ma'am?"

"Show Lord Ingemar out please, he has much to do and no time to waste."

"Yes ma'am. This way sir."

He scowls at me but follows her like a good boy.

With him gone I pick up my jacket and slip it on as my door opens to reveal Eumeleia, "Good, are you all ready to go? Where is your jacket?"

She lifts it from where she had it held behind her, "I am ready, mother. Why do we have to do this?"

"You are going to raise our family higher even than I have. While we are at this meeting you must appear to be a leader. I won't be able to guide you over much, though you can look to me for advice, as you should. If we do this right, you could be queen."

"Queen? How? The kings have never shown an interest in women and I don't want to marry any of them."

"Don't you worry about that, if you end up married to one it will be King Vincent and it will be temporary. Just do as I say and we will own this land."

"Own it? Mother, how?"

"You let me worry about that darling. Just you do as I say. Nothing and no one will stand in our way with our God blazing the path for us."

Valdís

I know this has to be a dream, but it feels so real. I am watching these women leave their homes under the dark moon. Some with children, mostly daughters unless they are very little. They steal away, a bag slung over their shoulders and a book or two in hand. They must be the witches of our land. I want to be there for them, but I have to do this.

Hekate's voice startles me, "You do. You are exactly where you must be right now. What you are seeing is what is happening at home." Suddenly we are at the castle door where the women have all gathered and I see the hidden guards watching to see what they do. One woman from the back of the group asks, "Has anyone tried knocking on the door?"

A murmur goes through the group and I hear some of them saying, "But it's so late, what if the kings are mad at being woke up?"

The one from the back marches around all of them and as she knocks on the door says, "Then they will deal with Her. She told us to come here and dammit, I am not standing outside all night to keep from waking the kings."

A guard opens the door almost immediately. They had to have been waiting for her to knock. He asks, "How can I help you ma'am?"

The woman gestures to include all the women as she says, "We need to speak with Valdís."

He looks out and I swear he pales before he gives himself a shake and says, "Please come in, you may wait here in the entry."

Hekate and I follow the group in to watch. Epaphras comes at a run, stopping dead at the sight of so many women and children. "Oh my. Yes, uh, do come in. Dear boy," he says turning to the guard with him, "lead these women to the throne room, I will get the kings."

I start to follow but Hekate stops me with a hand on my arm, "You simply needed to see this. The rest will work out as it should. Send the ones you have collected back as soon as it becomes evident that you have too many to hide or feed effectively." Her hand gets tighter on my arm, "Make sure no one else gets caught. Whatever you must do, no one else."

"Why is that so important? And does that mean I will be caught?"

"It has to happen this way. I can't say more than that.

Whatever happens, know I will be watching over you and doing what I can."

"I will do my best."

"I know you will. Now wake up."

My eyes fly open to see the sun rising. It is beautiful. I watch it as I cast the spell to find the next witch, ignoring the bad feeling in the pit of my stomach.

Seventeen

Valdís

"Chance, if you say one more word about going home before I have finished what I came here to do, I will hang you by the ankles. I learned the spell just for you and you are trying patience I don't have."

He growls and shoves his hands through his shaggy hair. The tie he uses to hold it back is currently on his wrist. I kind of hope he leaves it down. He is nice to look at when his lips aren't moving. "Valdís, this place isn't safe for any of you. You saw those women, they died at the hand of their own people. Who then wrote horrible things on and around their bodies! I have to make sure you get back to my brothers."

I smile a little as the sorrow in my heart swells. I think I have figured out what is coming and he is going to play a big part in it. "I know. And you will. For now, we have to collect as many as we can."

He snorts and crosses his arms, "As many as will believe you."

"I don't expect them all to believe. This place isn't nice to anyone that doesn't fit in and the familiar is safe to these women. We are strangers showing up at a time that is already terrifying for them. They've been raised to believe that witches are evil. Cursed. Damned to burn in their God's hell for all eternity. Which sounds awful to me, but I don't have any fear of it because I know that isn't what will happen to me. I know our Goddess. We talk pretty frequently compared to these people and their deity who it seems left them a book and rarely ever speaks to them. I know you don't like this, if it helps I don't either. I have to do it. I don't have a choice. Any more than you have a choice about feeding from people. I've seen you, when we are in the more populated areas or when someone is intent on catching one of my witches. I know you've been feeding on them. I don't care, I know you have to do it. And that is what this is like. I have to do it."

He groans, "How many more before we at least visit home? My brothers ask about you every day."

"I know. Tell them I love them and I will come back to them. Incidentally, why do you keep pointing your phone at me?"

He sits heavily on the ground, "I take pictures of you for them."

"You could have told me, I don't mind that."

"I like taking pictures when you don't know that's what I am doing. It makes the picture better."

I shrug, "Very well then." His scent is wafting over on

the breeze and I can't help but want him. Especially since I know he really is trying to take care of me. "Any ideas on how to convince these women?"

He laughs, "I don't think I am the one to ask about convincing women. I quit looking at them ages ago. I spend most of my time outside our land checking in on our companies or alone or doing terrible things that pay very well indeed. There are vast wildernesses that I wander for months, sometimes years if I can get someone to take my turn. No people, no anything but me and the pursuit of survival."

I lay back in the grass to look at the sky and hopefully not breathe in so much of him, "You must love it very much to spend so much time out there."

He lays back, his head next to mine. His scent surrounds me, making me long for things he doesn't want yet. I turn my head to look at him and find his eyes staring into mine as he says, "It's all just a way to cope with missing out on the one thing I crave more than anything else in the world."

My breath catches when he says that. I am afraid to ask but I have to know, "What is it you crave more than anything else in the world Chance?"

Dagma's shadow falls over my face, "Valdís, we're ready. The new one is sorted and as calm as she can be."

"Oh, um, ok." I get up and I can feel Chance doing the same, "Let's go ahead and get going then."

∼

Malic

"Are you certain we can't just go solve the problem?"

Knox sighs, "Malic. We have been through this. Cutting off heads does not solve problems. If anything it is likely to create more when Hekate finds out. Shit, she still isn't talking to us yet, I don't want to think about what she will do if you start trimming heads from bodies."

"Fine. Let's get this over with."

I follow him to the car and we ride down in the back seat, behaving like the kings we are meant to be. I hate it. I hate being in this stupid car. I really hate being dressed up to the point of discomfort. I hate all these expectations that we will behave a certain way. I don't want to cut off heads really. But I would like to walk away from it all. Every one of us, just take the people we work with and Valdís. Just leave this place. Leave the responsibility of it all.

No more worrying about the guards as they put a sign up in the place we speak from. No more concern about whether or not this will work well for us or be an entire shitshow. The car slows, we are nearly there. It comes to a stop and I look at Knox. He is as miserable as I am with this shit. "Come on, let's get this over with. I'll try not to make it more difficult on you. I know you don't want to do this any more than I do."

He sighs, "I don't and I miss Valdís. Let's go before I decide it isn't worth it."

The crowd cheers a lot more than I would have expected considering the things going on. Knox steps up to the podium and I stand back from him, a little to the right. Knox starts out by telling them that we are facing a grave threat from the Outsiders again and that is where it all starts to go wrong. Someone shouts, "The Outsiders are nothing more than an old tale used to scare children. If they ever existed, they are long dead by now!"

Knox tries to tell them that they are already being manipulated by the few left here, that are causing the strife in our land. Making them think that they are having a legal election. I shake my head as I can feel the people getting more upset. That same guy that was yelling about old tales is now saying that our Goddess is nothing more than a fairytale, that there wasn't a goddess to grant us kinghood. The only evidence they have is our existence and word. I can see Knox is angry now and about to respond. Then I hear Hekate's voice, by the look on Knox's face I am not the only one. She whispers to us, "Go home. Do not contradict them. Leave and go back to the castle, tend to the ones that need you and will accept your help."

Knox and I climb into the car as the crowd starts shouting about how we need to pay for our crimes.

Eumeleia

Tonight is the night! I have waited so long for him to even notice me. Now that my sister is gone, may she rot in the King's dungeon, he is finally seeing me. Mother has gone to bed early, she thinks I have no idea what other services her guards perform for her when she goes to bed early. Yuck.

Her being in her bedroom makes it all too easy for me to slip away unnoticed. One last check in the mirror to be sure I look perfect and demure for him. I don't want him thinking I am anything like my dirty sister. She is not marriage material for anyone, but I am. I have had dozens of proposals and turned them all down, for want of him.

Strolling through the mostly silent and deserted seeming house like I don't want to run out the door, I manage to avoid seeing anyone. Opening the front door is the most risky part, anyone catching me here will know that I am going out without approval. I have been an adult for so many years, but in this house that has counted for precious little as mother controls everything.

The fresh air smells delightful. I feel free. I know it will be short-lived, but at least I will get to see my beloved Pelos. If he were to decide he wanted to marry me, oh, I would defy even our God for him. I walk quickly to my destination, just around the corner to the community building.

He is waiting there when I round the corner of the building. His hair is slightly mussed and I see he has brought one of his father's vehicles. He is staring at the trees, facing away from me. I call out to him as I draw near, "Pelos, I wasn't sure you would come."

He smiles as he turns to face me, "I couldn't miss seeing you again. It is rare that I get to see you at all, and without your continual chaperone? Never. I wasn't sure at all that you would come to see me, that you could get out to see me."

I feel my cheeks heat, "I didn't know until that rally that

you had any interest in seeing me, with or without my chaperone."

He chuckles, "How could I not want to see you? Do you not know how beautiful you are? Any man would be lucky to find that you would deign to look upon him."

My heart races at his compliments. I never had a clue that he felt this way about me. His hand is soft and warm against my cheek. "I always thought you more interested in everyone else."

His hand leaves my face, "Like other men, I have needs and obligations. I was certain you were not the type of girl to fulfill my needs without the bonds of marriage between us and I had no desire to sully you in that way. I had always hoped that one day..."

"One day what?"

"That one day you would be mine. We would be wed and I could introduce you to all the things you had never experienced as a girl. That I could bring you to full womanhood."

I look away, my face aflame, "I would very much like that. But I don't know if it will be possible. My mother has grand plans for me and so long as I live with her, I have no choice but to go along with them."

He frowns and my heart breaks to have disappointed him, "What if you were to wed and no longer live under your mother's control?"

I struggle to keep from looking up at him with all my hope writ plain across my face, "Well, that would solve a great many problems and leave me only with the problem of how long it will be before she speaks to me again."

He takes my hands and draws me near, bringing them up to kiss with his incredibly soft lips, "And would you? Would you wed me? Leave your mother's home and become my bride? Foregoing the long courting you deserve simply because your mother would take you from me?"

Joy radiates from the center of my being, "I would love nothing more than to be your wife."

He wraps me up in his arms, lifting me and spinning me around, "Wonderful! I am the luckiest man on the planet!" When he sets me down he leaves his hands on my waist and I could combust from how nice it feels. I place my hands palm down on his chest. Taking advantage of the placement and stroking his chest just a little. He feels the perfect combination of firm and soft. I could get lost here but I am called back to reality as he says, "We must plan this, I will need to go apply for the license. Talk to the pastor. We will have a small ceremony and later a large reception to introduce you to our world properly."

"Oh yes! I would love that. When? Will we go right now?"

"Not yet my love. It takes time to do these things. We don't want your mother to say we kidnapped you."

My face falls, "No, we would not. And she would. But how will you let me know it is time?"

He smiles gently down at me, "We will meet here again in two days at this time. Can you get out?"

Worrying at my lower lip with my teeth I think about my mother's schedule. She doesn't have any evening appointments at all this week. She is likely to be going to bed early every night... "Yes, I should be able to. I will be late if she stays up, but not too late."

His smile blinds me, "Then it is done! I will see you here in two days time and let you know how our plans have progressed. Now, this night air is getting chill, let me drive you to the gate of your home. I wish I could pick you up from there, but I understand your mother is not amenable to you being the adult you obviously have been for a very long time."

"Oh, that would be lovely. Thank you, I was a little worried about walking home now that it is full dark."

In his vehicle, it is warm and soft music plays. The drive is much too short, he stops just before the opening to the gate, shutting off the headlights and turning to me, "May I have a single kiss before you go my love?"

I know my face must be bright red, it feels so hot as I whisper, "I would very much like that."

He leans toward me and I let my lashes flutter closed, his lips are softer even than they felt on my hands as he presses his lips to mine. The touch of his lips makes me hunger for more but before I can do more than think about it he pulls away.

I do my best to hide the sadness I feel at the loss as I open the door to get out. He watches as I walk in the gate and then I watch as he drives away, taking my heart with him.

Eighteen

Valdís

It is early morning as I sit looking out over the women I have collected. Everyone else is sleeping but I haven't been able to. When the last woman joined us something clicked and I knew it was time.

Time to send them all home and face whatever fate has in store for me. We are sheltered in a shallow valley and it is warm enough we didn't need to worry about a fire.

Even so, I feel it coming. I can almost feel eyes in the trees. Dagma wakes and comes to sit next to me. I look at her, "We have to send them home."

She nods, "It did seem the group was getting overlarge."

"It is. Do you think we could get Quorin, Katerine, and Kalina to go with them for training purposes?"

"They will, even if they don't like the idea of us being out here alone. But as good as you have gotten with your magic lately; and don't think I haven't noticed you practicing moving things. We really have very little to worry about."

"We have to send Chance out to hunt. He is scouting right now, his self-imposed guard duty."

"I know. I saw him on the far side of the ridge."

We watch the sun come up together and I wonder if she has guessed what is coming.

Chance comes over with the rising of the sun, "When will we move out today?"

"I think we need you to hunt us up some food first. We are completely out of supplies."

He nods, "And you promise you will stay here while I hunt?"

"I promise that I will not leave this place of my own volition without you."

His eyes narrow at my wording. "Very well. I'll go now."

We wait for ten minutes after he leaves. Then we get up and start waking everyone. Once they are up I open the portal to the castle. A soft breeze blows through, bringing the scents of home to me. A sigh escapes me and I turn, "Come ladies, let's get you going before my guard comes back." They chuckle as they start filing through the portal.

I groan when Knox and Malic barrel through the portal. They must have smelled me. It is so nice feeling the two of them wrap their arms around me, I could melt into this for a week or three. Malic is the first to say, "We were so worried for you. If it weren't for Chance sending us pictures, we still would be."

Knox asks, "Where is Chance?"

I smile, "I may have sent him hunting for all these people..."

He laughs and then sobers, "So you aren't coming home yet?"

"No, there are more for me to help. Right now, I need you to go back home and help the women I just sent there. Make sure I have a home to come back to. I need to finish this, to bring as many of these women home as I can before... before anything happens to them."

Malic studies me, "They've started killing them already, haven't they?"

I nod, looking away, "Some of them, we just got there too late. Some we were just minutes from being able to save them. They were still warm when we found them. You understand, right? You understand why I have to do this?"

Knox hugs me tightly, "Of course we do. We just want you safe. You make sure you come back to us."

I hug the both of them when Knox loosens his hold a little. I have to wonder if Hekate had anything to do with them being so willing to agree with me. Giving each of them a kiss, I send them through the portal. Every step they take I want to scream at them to go, I can feel the danger coming closer.

They get in the portal and turn to wave as I see the men crest the hill. My heart races as I send Dagma flying through the portal. My kings catch her and I shout, "I love you," a wave of my hand closes the portal before they can recover.

Nineteen

CHANCE

I don't know what she is planning but they have been pulling food in all this time and they damn sure don't need me to hunt. I leave the camp and circle around to be downwind so she can't smell me.

As soon as the portal opens, I understand. All the women we collected and three of those we-brought march into the portal. Knox and Malic run out, the reunion is tender and sweet. It makes me long for things I let go of a long time past. It makes me wish she cared for me like that. Fuck. I am going to have to admit that she is my queen. Hopefully she doesn't make me grovel too much because I might be willing at this point to actually grovel.

My brothers walk back into the portal. She is looking increasingly scared as they walk away, then she sends Dagma flying into them and closes the portal. I look in the direction she is watching and my heart drops as I see them.

There are too many, I can't fight them and ensure that she lives.

Fuck! I got distracted and now she is surrounded by these people. They are taunting her, asking who will save her and calling her witch. Dawning realizations begin slamming into my mind. She spent all the time we have been here practicing throwing things around. She knew something was coming and wanted to make sure no one was caught with her. She knew and sent me away. She knew and left herself open to make sure all of us were free. The pain shoots through a heart I thought was dead all this time. I have to save her.

She says nothing to them as they taunt her. One pulls out a billy club and she looks directly at me with her big, sad eyes right before they knock her out. Everything in me wants to murder them all right now. I have to wait. If I go now, they will kill her when they see me. Long before I can get to them.

My phone has been going off for several long minutes I pull it out of my pocket as I watch one of them throw her roughly over their shoulder. He is dying slowly. Well, maybe not slowly, but definitely painfully. The men walk back in the direction they came from, so slowly I could catch up if I ignored them for an hour. I finally look at my phone; I have a lot of missed calls from Knox and Malic, along with messages.

Where are you?

What is happening?

Do you have eyes on her?

Chance, what the hell is going on?

I saw everything. Am in pursuit. Will update.

Shoving the phone in my pocket I take off, following these dead men carrying my queen.

Twenty

Valdís

There is a hand on my face. It reeks. Who the fuck is touching me? My mind still screaming, I lash out with my hands, hitting something soft and shoving as hard as I can from here.

Opening my eyes I see an old man in very fancy robes on the floor. Bile rises in my throat at the thought of him touching me. I hear him grunt as another man in a dark uniform helps him to stand. My head feels like it's recently been used as a kickball, but I keep my eyes on them. The old man nods at the one in uniform and he walks over and kicks me hard.

The impact makes me throw up all over their pretty floor and it really does nothing for my headache either. I finally sit myself up and I see that I have bled all over this floor. Holding myself up on my arms as I am too weak to go further just yet, I wonder how crazed will this make Chance when he gets here.

I caught the scent of him when the wind shifted after they first got to the valley. I know he was watching. He is way too smart for my lame hunting excuse. I put my hand in the blood and start trying to get up. The uniformed one grabs my other arm, wrenching it painfully as he snatches me to my feet. Oh, I don't like the way the room is spinning, I don't like it at all. I may just throw up again if this doesn't go away pretty quickly. The man is pulling me toward a chair but nothing is working quite right and then he freezes as a loud noise reaches us. The old man says, "Bring her with us."

My head is clearing as the old man shuffles to a wall and pushes a section of it, causing a door to slide back and into the wall. I keep stumbling, putting my bloody hand on the wall. I can't do much, but I can leave a bloody damn trail.

I stumble and touch the wall all the way through the tunnel. The uniform is growing annoyed but what do I care? They are going to hurt me anyway, might as well fuck with them. See if they can do any worse than growing up with Eirene.

The old man starts complaining, "Why didn't you say you would have someone coming after you? Witches! Evil creatures the lot of you!"

I can't help but bark a sharp laugh. It makes my head pound, but what a fucking moron. I'm not telling him shit after his people kidnapped me. What the fuck kind of people does he usually deal with anyway?

We emerge into sunlight so bright it causes pain to

radiate from my eyes throughout my skull. I am squinting to see as the old man climbs into the back seat of a vehicle. He gets seated and uniform shoves me at the open door. I throw my hands out, leaving a bloody handprint on the side of the car. The uniform puts a hand on my back and shoves again, making me fall into the vehicle. He shoves me further in and climbs in himself. I think I have rug burn on my cheek. They let me lay there as the vehicles starts to move.

Where are you Chance?

Chance

I am behind them as they take her into the compound. The security is relatively lax. I see no cameras and they have more than one tree close enough for me to climb it and watch them before I drop down onto their wall. They never once look up. What is that? Do I smell fuel? Are they keeping fuel in this place?

Well, this is going to be a lot more fun now.

I see the fuel is next to the wall here, just a little to my right. Closer to one of their outbuildings. The wind shifts and I can smell her, the scent is faint but there. Hopping down off the wall I walk up to the first person I see. A man in the robes of a cultist. Grabbing his robe at the neck and snatching him over to face me, I smile as he screams. "You will all scream for mercy before I kill you."

He screams louder and men are running at me as I sink my teeth into that juicy artery beating so fast to match his racing heart. His blood slakes my thirst and invigorates me.

Ripping away from him and leaving his throat gaping, I toss his body at a guard, sending them both flying at the outbuilding that is too small to have people in it.

Making it safe to burn.

More men are reaching me, I curl my fingers and rip the throat out of one, continuing the swing and making a bloody fist to hit another, causing him to sail a few feet away before landing on the pavement. One man stood back and shot me. Not the most pleasant feeling ever. I grabbed one of the others attacking me and held him in front of me as I drank the life from him. Then I threw him at the guy still trying to shoot me.

I need to quit playing and find her. Oh but wait. There is the guy that hit her with a billy club and threw her over his shoulder. He is going in the fuel barrel. I wait as he stalks closer with his gun drawn, pointed at me. His eyes though, his eyes are on his companions littering the ground. His horror grows and he isn't paying attention as he draws closer to me. Using my speed I close the short distance between us, taking his gun from him and wrapping my arm around his neck. "Say, do you have a lighter?"

The man just screams in answer, guess not. I check his pockets and he really doesn't. Dragging him along with me I check the other bodies. A-ha! A lighter. What do you know? The guy that shot me is a smoker.

This guy I am dragging along has got a hell of a set of lungs on him. We get to the fuel barrel and I tip it on its side, rolling it closer to the building. The guy switches from screaming to begging for his life now.

I figure he is ready to talk so I ask him, "Where is the woman you took?"

"Inside. She is inside with the cardinal!"

"Good, good. What is he planning to do with her?"

The guy starts crying, "Don't make me tell you that. You are just going to kill me anyway. I don't want it to hurt."

"Ok, I understand. You tell me and I will kill you quick, before I set everything on fire."

"Oh god save me, please, I was just doing what I was told."

I smile, "Oh I know. I know the cult you work for, the cowards all of you are. Your god won't save you from me. Now, fire or a quick death?"

"You promise it will be quick? No matter what I tell you?"

A growl erupts from me. I know this is going to be more than I am prepared to hear. "Yes. As long as you get on with it."

He is shaking hard as he tells me, "They are going to run tests on her, to find a way to take her power for the order. If they can't do that, they are going to breed her."

Rage clouds my mind and I see only red as I snap his neck. Lifting him high I toss him at the fuel barrel, busting it and getting fuel all over him. I watch the fuel run downhill toward the little outbuilding. A flick of the lighter and a ball of fire ignites in front of me. The man is burning and I walk away to grab the two I drank from to put in the fire. Suddenly, I am thrown to the ground by an explosion that rocks the compound. Well, if they didn't know I was here before, they do now. I look back, the outbuilding is now an inferno. Makes this easier.

Grabbing one body I toss him at the flames, and then the same with the other before heading toward the door to the main building.

Inside, I can smell the cleaning fluids they have used to wash away her scent. A faint aroma of her blood lingers. My rage grows as I follow my nose through the maze of hallways. Finally, I come to the door where her scent is strongest and I force the knob to turn, breaking the lock. I open the door gently, I don't want to hit her, my queen. As soon as I open the door though, the scent of her blood and vomit overwhelms my senses and I roar as I see the puddle of blood next to the vomit. They will pay.

No one is left in the room and I turn to leave but stop when I see the blood on the wall. Crossing the room I study the print. It is cut off cleanly. This is her blood, and if I had to guess, her hand. Is my queen leaving me a trail of breadcrumbs? I lean in close to the wall and close my eyes to focus on my sense of smell. It doesn't take long to find the spot that smells of a man. Opening my eyes I press on that spot. A door opens, revealing the rest of the hand print, it is hers. I jog down the hall, I can smell the spots where she has touched the wall with her bloody hand. She has to still be bleeding for there to be so much. If those fools kill her, their deaths will be incredibly slow. I'll take them home.

I emerge into the sunlight and squint as my eyes adjust. I see drops of her blood on the pavement, and a spot of red on the roof of the car driving away. Another car is here, I go to it and open the door. I have to waste precious time trying to find the keys, hidden in a compartment under the dash.

When I turn the car on, a screen lights up, showing various dots on the map. Most are unmoving. One appears to indicate this car. Another is speeding away from this one. That's got to be her.

I see the house catching fire as I pull away. Good. The sun is setting as I pull out my phone and message Malic,

Just missed her. Still in pursuit. Leads are good. Will have her back soon. She is injured, can Dagma travel here?

Twenty-One

KNOX

How are there so many? And half of them from here? I ask myself for the fiftieth or so time since Valdís added to the count yesterday. Biting my lip I shove the pain down again. "Dagma, is there a way for you all to, I don't know, purify the contaminated food? The preservations spells should have it still good, if we can get that edible..."

She nods, "Then it would help keep our ever-growing crowd fed till we get things situated regarding that stupid election."

"Exactly. At least until Gage or Vincent arrives with food. We had not planned for something like this."

She laughs, "No one plans for these things. They happen and we deal with them the best we can. We are still testing everyone to see what they are best at. It may be possible that we can create a spell that would do the trick. If it is a spell, then we can get the food right quickly. We will have to test it though. Perhaps we can put a light paste of flour on someone's skin. The delivery that way is slow and I can heal them from that before they die if the spell doesn't work."

"Excellent idea. Let me know how that goes. And please do work on it as soon as possible."

She smiles, "Don't you worry, we'll find a way."

"Oh, there are some other food stuffs from the first attempted poisoning. The guards can show you where it is."

"Don't you worry King Knox, we'll get this sorted." She marches out looking very determined.

Walking out of my office, the heartbreak and rage hit me again, so strong it stops me in my tracks. How am I supposed to manage when she is the reason my heart beats again? I feel the heartbreak taking over and I head for Valdís's room. Maybe I can still smell her in there. At the very least I can cry in private.

By the time I make it into her room, the tears are already flowing.

I sit down on the couch she usually sat in to read and pick up the pillow, holding it to my face and breathing in the remnants of her scent. The tears flow faster and I pull the pillow away to keep from soaking it and erasing her scent. It just hurts so much that she is probably hurting right now. I want to go help her, help Chance free her. But she asked me to stay and take care of things here. I don't know how Malic is managing it.

The tears just keep coming, the hurt is not easing. In desperation, I whisper, "Hekate, help me. Please."

An image of her appears before me and she asks, "What do you need, my warrior king?"

"I need to go help find her. Make sure she is safe, or bring her to safety. Like she did for us. She knew they were coming and sacrificed herself to save us, to make sure none of us were caught with her. Tell me what to do. How to ease this pain? I am lost without her."

Hekate sighs and smiles down at me, "You are not lost, you are doing exactly what she asked you to do. And that is what you must do. She is leading with her heart in ways you aren't capable of right now. This pain, this pain is worse for you right now because you stopped feeling anything for so long. That's part of what makes her so special. Deny it as she might, her heart has remained open even with all she has been through. She cares so much for everyone. Even when she tries to hate them, she still cares. Take care of the ones she collected. Help Chance as you can from here. Tell Malic that I know what he is planning and if he leaves my island I will put him back here myself." She sighs and the image sits across from me, "These things must happen. She wouldn't want you to know this but, she knew what was coming. She knew who, or at least what kind of people were coming. Before everything happened, she figured it all out. And then made the choice that she would do or suffer, whatever had to happen in order to save everyone. She knew Chance didn't actually go hunting. She has faith in him and you should too. He is working to rescue her even now. My hunter will not give up his pursuit. She will come back. I am with her even now, watching over her. Doing what I can."

"I don't like it. I would rather we take the risks."

"I know you would. You will need to trust your queen to do this. Trust in her strength."

"I will. I don't like it. But I will."

Her image fades away as she says, "I know. Be well, Knox."

~

Malic

The procession of guards and food through the garage and into the castle has been going for half an hour already. Epaphras has been ticking off boxes as they go by. I ask him, "How long do we have?"

He shrugs, "Perhaps two weeks? Women keep showing up at the door, adding to our numbers."

"How long before Gage or Vincent arrives?"

"Gage is loading right now. He should arrive within the next week or so, providing the waters cooperate."

"Good, and what we have should last at least that long."

"Yes. Longer still if what Knox is talking to the witches about works."

"What is Knox asking the witches to do?"

From behind me, Knox says, "Purify the tainted food. Malic, can I talk to you in private for just a moment?"

He looks less strained than he has since Valdís was taken. What happened? I check my phone, nothing new since Chance's last message. We walk to the far side of the garage from where everything is happening, "What's going on Knox?"

He gives a half smile, "Always so suspicious. You can't

go. That's what's happening. **She** said you can't go. More to the point Hekate said if you try to go she will put you back on her island herself."

"What do you mean Hekate said that? She hasn't talked to any of us in so long I barely recall her voice!"

"Well, **She** talked to me today. I went to Valdís's room because I was hurting and I just asked her to help. Next thing I know **She** is there and talking to me."

My heart breaks as Knox tells me the rest of what Hekate said about Valdís. I shove a hand thru my hair, "She specifically said I cannot go?"

He nods, "She looked annoyed about it. She might break your boat over this. But she said we can help Chance from here. We need to think outside of the usual, how can we help? What can we arrange to make things easier for him to save her? Can we drop supplies off to him? Something else? Get him some mercenaries to help?"

"Fine. I'll check in with Chance and see what we can do. When will the witches know if what they are doing works or not?"

He shrugs, "It looked like Dagma was going to work on it right then. So maybe very soon, maybe not. Maybe it won't work at all."

"That's the most helpful of answers, Knox."

He grins at me, "It's what I have right now. I have some things to go do. See you at dinner?"

"I guess you will since I'm not fucking well going anywhere."

❧

Ingemar

The vote happened today. I stayed away from the polling place, being a candidate. But now it is late in the evening and the votes have been counted. Walking into the polling place I see Lord's Judda and Kleitos. Lord Judda smiles widely, "Congratulations my King! You have won the vote."

"Excellent."

Lord Kleitos smirks, "We only had to throw out about three-quarters of the votes from the only two polling places we set up to ensure that you won. Terribly popular aren't you?"

Narrowing my eyes I tell him, "It never mattered whether or not the vote actually went my way. This was always about deposing the kings. My popularity doesn't matter. Who they actually voted for doesn't matter."

He chuckles, "It might if people start talking to each other about who they voted for."

"By the time they figure it out, we will have fully taken over and it won't matter." Turning to Lord Judda I ask, "Have you scheduled the parade? We will be ending it at the king's podium in the central square, yes?"

"We will. The cars are waiting out back and word has been spread. People should be starting to line the streets of the route. We can go whenever you are ready."

"Let us not keep the people waiting."

The parade is small, only three vehicles. All of them have their tops down, mine is the middle vehicle. Seating myself up where everyone can see me I work on my smile, trying to ensure that it looks as sincere as possible. Pelos is conspicuously absent but that is fine. He has been less than useful since his mother's passing. The cars start rolling slowly through the route. Sitting up tall and proud I wave at the people that have come out to watch us go by. There aren't many women out watching and the ones that are seem angry. Perhaps things are already changing to reflect the new power dynamic. This is good. Women should be more concerned with their homes.

Lives here will be greatly improved with a better definition of the roles of men and women. The parade is slow but relatively short and once we arrive at the kings podium I see a crowd, with more joining. The crowd is predominantly male, including the ones joining. I see that one of the priests from a local temple is here, and they have a crown? I spin to look at Lord Judda and he grins. This is perfect. I am to be crowned here before this crowd by our local clergy.

I never dreamed anything like this could happen in a million years. Walking slowly up the stairs to the platform, I am gratified to hear cheers coming from the crowd. The ceremony to crown me is short, the clergyman only telling everyone that what is chosen by her people is what the Goddess herself ordains as she wants only for us to be happy and safe.

Once the ceremony is over I move forward to the podium and a great cheer rises. Smiling and gesturing for them to calm down I wait to speak. Once there is silence I begin, "My people, I stand before you as the first, but not last, king chosen by the people for the people. I am honored to have been chosen by you and I will do my best to ensure the men of this kingdom continue to know they made the right choice for our land.

Though you have spoken, have chosen your king, the fight is not over. We must wrest this land from the tyranny of its former rulers who squat in the castle even now, refusing to stop their depredations of our people. Many of you have recently lost wives and daughters to the kings, their hunger for flesh has returned and it is only our women that slake their sinful thirst for blood.

As they go missing our people grow closer and closer to extinction. We cannot allow this to happen. This is why we are building an army to remove the false kings from our land once and for all. We need strong young men along with older men of thought and action. Any true patriots of our land wishing to join in deposing the false kings, report to my home and start your training. You heroes are what this country needs to stop our people from dying out, leaving our lands cold and empty."

The cheers are loud and ecstatic. I notice a great many starting toward my home. Perfect.

Twenty-Two

Valdís

We arrive at a building and uniform guy drags me out of the car. He tries to get me to stand but I am so dizzy, the world just doesn't want to sit still. The old man tells him, "Pick her up. We don't want her to die before we can get the power from her."

My stomach drops when he says that. How do they think they are going to get my power from me? Are they really so stupid they think that anything has changed since the last time they tried to take power from the witches? Morons. Keeping my eyes mostly closed I am able to focus a bit and watch. They take me through white corridors that seem endless. Another uniform guy is standing in front of a door. He opens it and the old man enters, the uniform guy carrying me follows after. It smells harsh, like a type of disinfectant in here. It burns my eyes and nose a little at first.

There is another man in here wearing a long white coat.

I don't know why but he terrifies me. Then the old man says, "We need her kept compliant. Can you do that or do I need to call someone else?"

The man smiles and I want to hide. My head is so messed up I don't know if I could find my magic, much less whether I could do anything with it if I did. He brings out a syringe filled with something. The guard's arms tighten around me as white coat draws near. Oh goddess, what is he going to do to me? He taps the syringe and pushes out a tiny amount of liquid. Quick as a snake he stabs me in the arm with it and presses the plunger.

I bite my lip from the pain. I can feel it spreading through my body. It feels thick, and slimy. It makes my limbs and my eyes feel so heavy. My mind is still as awake as before. Which isn't much at this point, but I feel it succumbing to this drug as well. The guard is carrying me somewhere, he lays me down on a floor. I hear the old man telling someone, clean this blood off of her. The disgusting creatures that rule them can smell it for a long way. I believe there is one here as my personal compound was attacked."

I wake up a short time later laying on my back and I can smell antiseptic on me. My limbs are still heavy but I reach up and touch my head. There is a bandage over the cut. Working my fingers under the edge and pulling it ever so slowly, I manage to remove it. The skin underneath the bandage feels slightly scabbed over when I get my hand back to it. I pick at it until I feel a sharp pain and the sensation of liquid running across my scalp. I let my hand fall to the floor again, exhausted. The darkness welcomes me back into its sweet embrace as I wonder, where is he?

It seems like Chance will never find me. I can almost feel him until they stab me with another syringe. The drug they give me keeps my mind feeling like it is clad in mounds of gauze. I try to lift my hand to the cut on my head, to make sure the blood scent is fresh. A strange sound, clinks and my hand stops, falling back to the floor. It's a struggle to open my eyes but I manage it and I see my wrists are wrapped in metal cuffs attached to chains. How am I going to make sure Chance can find me if I can't get rid of the bandage and make it bleed again? Hot tears slip down my face, I want to sob. The sensation of a hand on my face startles me. Forcing my eyes open I see the shadowy form of a woman. I feel like I should recognize her. She whispers, "I am here, little one. I will remove the bandage. And make the man open the window so Chance can find you."

Her hands are soft and kind as she removes the bandage. A sharp pain and I feel the now familiar sensation of blood running down my scalp. A sigh escapes me as she smoothes the hair back from my face. She is with me even when the man stabs my thigh. I wonder how he got through my pants, I would swear I was wearing thick jeans. Maybe I imagined that? I hate that the drugs make it so I can't feel Chance anymore. Where are you Chance?

The woman whispers, "He is coming. He will have you soon. Even now, the scent of your blood is making him more determined to find his way to you."

The sound of her voice is soothing and I wonder why I don't recognize her. "Don't. Let. Them. See. You. Stay.

With. Me." Getting the words out felt like such work. My tongue is thick and doesn't want to form words like it should.

The woman smiles down, "Don't worry my Valdís, they won't see me and I will be here with you until you leave this place."

"Promise?"

"I promise. If I have to break all the rules I will do so, but I am staying with you. I'm so sorry you had to be here at all. I would have done it any other way if I could."

I try to nod but the drug is starting to work and nothing happens.

~

Chance

I have been watching the building where I believe they are keeping her for days. The old man that I smelled in that room goes in there every day with his guard. The building is squat, and has precious few windows. The windows that are there are heavily tinted and impossible to see through. They don't appear to be the type that open very far either.

The old man enters a code every time he goes into the building. Happily, Knox and Malic arranged for some supplies to come to me and included a very good set of binoculars. His code has been the same every time he has gone in there. I am watching him leave when suddenly I smell her. The breeze carries the sweet scent of her blood. Binoculars up to my eyes I study the building. There! The one window on the right side of the building is open, probably as far as it will go. Useless as an entry point but now I know which direction to head when I get inside the building. She shouldn't still be bleeding. Why is she still bleeding? I have to get her out of there. Tonight, darkness falls in a couple hours. Only two guards once everyone from the day shift leaves. They probably think they are safe since no one has come for her yet.

I pull out my phone and call Malic, he answers before the first ring finishes, "Have you got her yet?"

"No, going in tonight. I had to make sure I could get her without causing further damage. Now I know roughly where she is in the building. I called because I want to turn this building into rubble when I get her out. I spend most of my time out in the wilderness so I don't know people."

"But I do. I'll send a team to you. Give me your coordinates. They will arrive within the hour, ready to go."

"Good. Make sure they know it's a stealth mission and we go in after darkness falls."

"They aren't amateurs. What's the security like?"

"They have a camera pointing at the door. A coded door, only one entrance. The building is one floor but appears to be concrete blocks. Few windows and they don't appear to be wired but also don't open more than an inch or so."

"Ok. Be watching for my men."

"I will. And I'll send a picture as soon as I get her to the safe house."

I move further away from the building and send Malic my coordinates. Settling into a tree I lift the binoculars to my eyes and watch.

The men arrived faster even than Malic said. I don't know where they parked but they walked up from the opposite direction of the building. I watch them as they draw closer, continually scanning the area. When they are under my tree the leader looks up and says, "I hope you're Chance. I don't like killing civilians."

I laugh, "I am. I have a good vantage point if you would like to scope out the place. We have another hour or so before the sun sets."

He climbs up into the tree with me, positioning himself on a limb to the left of me. He brings his binoculars up and studies the building in silence. "Will you need help on the inside?"

"No, only two guards. I have the old man's code memorized, shouldn't be any problems with an alarm."

"Good. We'll set up while you retrieve your package. When you have cleared, we'll all return to the vehicles, your brother sent you one too. This place will blow about the time we get to the cars. Will you be able to move fast carrying your package or will you need an assist?"

"I can keep up."

"Good. Your brother sent some keys, they are in the glove box. He said you would know what they were for."

"I do."

Easing back against the trunk of the tree, I settle in to wait for the cover of darkness.

We watch as people exit the building. I point to the man in the lab coat as he leaves, "That one. Bring him to me and you all will get a bonus."

The man on the limb next to mine looks at me and whispers down to his guys. I watch two of them take a vehicle from the parking lot and follow the man away from the building. He turns his head to me, "He will be in the trunk of your vehicle, unconscious and well-trussed."

Nodding, I pull out my phone and message my brother to give the men a bonus for delivering the scientist that has had access to her all this time and smells of her when he leaves the building.

The man next to me gets a notification on his phone and his eyes pop as he inhales sharply. "That's a helluva bonus!"

"My brothers and I are appreciative. It is dark enough now. I'm going in."

He nods as I swing my body down to hang from the branch until I let go, landing lightly on the grass beneath. Instead of sneaking I walk across the lot like I have been there a thousand times. Keeping my face turned away from the camera I use the keypad, typing in the old man's code. The light flashes green and I push the door open. Inside, there are small lights lining the halls giving me plenty to see by. I hear a guard walking a circuit ahead of me, heading in the general direction I need to go. I can smell her. Smell her blood. The animal in me wants to tear this place to shreds until I find her. I take a few slow breaths, reminding myself that I have to go slow for her. That's the only way to save her is to be methodical. We don't hunt in a blind panic.

I tread lightly to the first door. There is a woman in a cage in there, but it isn't her. I'll get her out on the way back through. Another room. Another woman. And on and on. Seven doors and each one has a woman in a cage. What are they doing here? Why do they have women in cages... suddenly I remember why we were here to begin with. These women are all witches. I would bet on it. Room eight is another woman. Room nine, this is where she is. I can smell her through the door. I can also hear one of the guards coming. Back to the corner I turned moments ago and I wait for him, leaning one shoulder against the wall. As he comes even with me I say, "You really aren't very good at this are you?"

The guy drops to the ground and starts crying, "Please don't hurt me. This was supposed to be easy, I'm only here for the paycheck." As he snivels he unhooks his belt and drops it away from himself, all his gear, including the walkie on it. I am confused as I watch him, he doesn't seem to be one of them. They hire out for the night shift? He turns out his pockets, his cell goes clattering across the floor. "Please, I swear I won't tell anyone. I just want to live. It isn't right what they do to these women anyway. I'll help you, but please don't kill me. It's my brother in the office, we just took the job to get by. Please, please...."

"Stand up." The man gets to his feet, making no move to even touch any of his things. "Will your brother help too? Do either of you have any loyalty to this organization?"

He laughs through his tears, "We are paid minimum wage and treated like dogs."

"So you need money. Is your loyalty for sale? I have a job for you and it will pay enough that you never have to come back here again."

"For that much, you could have my soul. What do you need?"

"Let's get your brother with us first." We walk to the control room for all of the building. He opens the door and speaks quietly to his brother and I watch from the shadows as he takes off his belt and sets his phone on the counter. I ask them, "How many women are in this building?"

The one from the control room says, "Thirteen. Always thirteen."

His brother looks at him, "Artie, how do you know that?"

Artie says, "Because I'm nosy as hell and good on the computer. And these guys don't lock shit up except the building itself."

I smile, "Artie, I appreciate that. Why always thirteen?"

Now his face drops and he tugs at his collar, "They, um, they think the women are witches and they want to take their power for themselves. They believe having thirteen is the key."

I nod, biting my lower lip, "Ok. Artie, can you get everything on a jump drive for me?"

Now he blushes, "I um. Hm. I may have already put it on a drive in the hopes that it would protect us when we leave here."

His brother says, "What? Why would we need protection?"

"Because I saw the real handbook, Darnell. They don't

let people quit once they have been inside the building. Nobody leaves the organization."

Darnell pales under his dark skin and looks back at me, "Mister, you get us out of here and we'll go wherever you go."

Artie nods his agreement and I shrug, "Have you got the keys to the women's cages?" Darnell says he does and opens a drawer, pulling out a ring of keys. "Are they all drugged?"

Artie says, "No. Just the one. She keeps hurting herself and they keep her drugged to try and stop that."

I nod, gritting my teeth. "Here is what we are going to do. You are going to give me the key to the one that is drugged. Then I want you to go get the other women out of their cages and wait for me near the door. Got it?"

Darnell doesn't speak, just pulls one key off the ring and leads Artie out of the office. They are quick and efficient as they get the women out and lead them to the next. I wait for them to round the corner before I enter her room. Her cage is steel bars whereas the other women had simple chain link spaces. Fumbling with the key I unlock the door of her cage. Her eyes fly open when the door clanks. She begins to whimper and I move to her quickly. "Sh, it's okay, princess. I'm here. I've got you. I'm going to take you away from here. They'll never touch you again."

Her eyes are so dilated, and she whispers, "Chance?"

Scooping her up I say, "It's me. Just hang on, let's get you home and we'll talk then."

"Oh Chance, I'm so glad you found me." Her eyes droop and close as her head falls back. If I see that old man again I will end him. Then I remember the scientist in the trunk and that makes me smile as I carry her thru the hall. Near the door I see Darnell, Artie, and twelve women waiting. "Listen up. We are going to march away from here and to a vehicle. Artie, Darnell, do you have a vehicle?" They nod and Artie holds up a single finger. "Good. Drive it to the other side of the green space, our vehicle is waiting there. We weren't counting on so many. We'll need your vehicle to help get everyone to the safe house."

Darnell says, "Artie, go with them. I'll get the car."

Artie nods and I look to the women, "I know you are probably terrified, and I'm sorry for that. I came here for her but she would be mad if I left you all behind and would insist on coming back. So you are all coming to the safe house and we'll make sure that you are kept safe. Just follow me, ok?"

The women all nod and I walk past them, one of the women runs in front of me to open the door, I tell her, "Thank you." She nods and we walk out into the night.

Twenty-Three

CHANCE

The first ring barely finishes before Malic answers, "How is she?"

"She's still out. The drugs they have been giving her are still in her system. The scientist says it will take time for them to be fully filtered out because they were dosing her much more often than was strictly necessary."

I can hear Malic's teeth grind over the connection. He says, "Will you be bringing the scientist home with you?"

I grin, "If you would like him as a present, say the word my brother. His life is yours. That isn't all I called to talk about though. There is a lot more."

"Bring him to me. What else?"

"They are collecting witches. They have this hair-brained idea that with thirteen of them, they could somehow take their power from them for the church."

"There were other witches there?"

"There were. I brought the other twelve with us. Plus

two security guards because they were easily bought. I needed the help. And I felt sorry for them if I am honest."

"Fair enough. They coming home with you?"

"The witches, yes. The guards? I need to ask them but they said something about going where I go so I think they will. Oh, we have a drive with information from their terminal at that location. From what I understand, they keep all the terminals fully updated as they only go online once a day."

"Good. Were they all swept for bugs?"

"They were. As well as being thoroughly searched the guard's car was also swept and searched. The guys you sent said that there was evidence that they have been living in their vehicle for quite some time."

"I see. Well, bring them home with you and we'll see if anything appears on their ears. I mean, they could be descendants. Or from one of the few countries that weren't in the fight. If they are, we'll keep them. If not, we can pay them well and set them up somewhere else."

"Good. They behave like they are not of the Outsiders, genuinely caring of each other for one. Besides that, since they switched sides they have been really forthcoming about everything. They are the only living relatives they have. Everyone else in their family is dead. Since that building burned to char with a lot of bodies in it, everyone here likely thinks they are dead. The church thinks all the women died in there as well."

"Good. Where did they find fifteen bodies to put in there?"

"That's not my business and I didn't ask. I hear her stirring. I've got to go."

"Send me a picture!"

"I will."

Valdís

I hear noises. Maybe voices? Are there people here? Where am I? This doesn't feel like the floor. My eyes don't want to open yet, I open my hands to feel what I can. My arms aren't completely getting the message just yet but it seems like maybe a bed. How? The voices do sound like women and men.

I have to open my eyes. Panic is starting to set in as they feel so heavy. I try to breathe slower. Maybe if I start working on getting motion back to everything else I can convince my eyes to open. I curl my fingers again. Stretch them back out. Toes. Feet. Hands. I go through all my body parts and get them to respond before I bring my hands up to my face. Which is when I realize I have a blanket over my face. Curling my fingers around the blanket I pull it down slowly, letting the light bathe my face before I try to open my eyes again. This time they respond and though they feel grainy and dry, they open. And blink a lot. By the time moisture has returned to my eyes and I open them, there is someone standing at the foot of the bed I lay in. My heart starts to race as I realize it is Chance. I croak out, "Am I dead?"

He walks around to the side of the bed and sits down,

"You are not dead. Can I help you sit up and drink some water?"

"Yes please, I don't think I could accomplish that on my own." His hands are gentle as he slips them under my arms and slowly eases me up into a sitting position. I am exhausted from someone else pulling me into an upright position. This is so ridiculous. He brings a glass of water near me and gets the straw in it angled so I only need to tip my head and open my lips to drink from it. The water feels amazing, like it is rinsing away grit and ick all the way down.

After I have had my fill he sets it back on the table and asks, "How are you feeling?"

"Disgusting. Gross. Weak. Like I want to shower for a month or two. What happened? I remember letting them capture me, I remember being taken to the car and arriving at a building. Most things after that are kind of blank."

He nods as a muscle in his jaw ticks, "They were drugging you heavily. They said that it was to keep you from injuring yourself because you kept making yourself bleed. They were concerned you would die. You weren't trying to hurt yourself, were you?"

"No! I know how much the scent of my blood affects your brothers; I figured it was likely to do the same for you. It was my way of helping you find me."

"Knew I was coming for you, eh?"

I smile at him, or try to, "I did. And so did she."

His brows shoot up, "She?"

"Hekate. She was with me a lot. The longer I am awake the more it is all coming back to me. She said you were coming, and she helped me pick at the wound to make sure that you found me."

"Of course she did. Did you know they were coming?" Looking away from him I nod. "You said let them. Why did you let them capture you?"

"Are you sure you want to know?" He nods, eyes burning into me as that muscle ticks like crazy. I want to smooth it, but I don't know if he would welcome my touch. "Very well. I let them because I finally understood what she meant. She told me to make sure they didn't capture anyone else. It would all fall apart if they did. She also said she wished it could be any other way or something like that. My head is still fuzzy. I had figured it out while we were traveling. That morning, that morning just felt bad. Like a storm building and you just know it's going to rip through everything. I was so scared when Knox and Malic came running through the portal. I was certain I had it figured out, and they had to go back. Them being there was sort of perfect though, because there was someone to catch Dagma. I knew you wouldn't go far since I had the feeling you weren't buying my story, but you had to be out of the way. And safe."

A low grumble rolls out from his chest before he says, "I don't like it. Don't do it again. You can't help anyone if you die."

I study his face, "You found out what they wanted to do, didn't you?" He nods. "It won't work. They can't take my power from me."

"No, but they can kill you and the other twelve women they want to strip power from in whatever fucked up fantasy they have where thirteen witches together means that they can take your powers."

"Wait, did they have other women there?" He shakes his head yes and I start to panic, "Did you bring them too? Tell me you saved them too!"

He smiles ruefully, "I knew you would make me go back for them if I didn't. Not that I particularly wanted to leave them, they just weren't my cause for being there. I brought them and I poached their night security. Then we had the building turned into rubble. It isn't the only one they had, but it is one they no longer have."

"Good." I sigh in relief and then I remember I still have that place on me. "I need a shower. I want to wash that place off of me." My face heats as I study my lap, "Could, um, hm. Could you help me?"

I wait as the silence stretches and panic sets in, "Never, uhm, never mind. I can wait. Or get someone else to help me or—" a single finger presses against my lips and I lift my eyes to meet his.

"I would be honored to help. I wasn't trying to find a way to say no, I was trying to control my reaction to being asked."

He withdraws his finger from lips that are feeling a tingly sort of feeling. Oh no. This is probably going to be torture for him. If my body is responding to him shushing me... "You don't have to. I am still really weak and," oh man, there goes my face again, "as much as I don't like to admit it currently, you touching me is likely to ignite fires I can't do anything about right now. I know you guys have that really sensitive sense of smell going for you. It seems to be difficult—"

He puts his arms under my knees and behind my torso, lifting me out of the bed with ease. "I am fully aware of what my touch does to you, it does the same when you are sleeping. I am also fully capable of maintaining my self-control. Even when it is difficult. You don't worry about it, I can help you shower without attacking you even if your scent does cause a raging hard-on."

Oh, that didn't help. I have to think about something else. What? Maybe home? Yes. Home and my mom. Who may not be entirely happy about my throwing her through the portal. At least Knox and Malic were there. Oh, I miss them. My core clenches in agreement, sending shivers through my body. That may not be the way to go either. Chance sets me on my feet slowly, leaning me against a wall and keeping a hand pressed firmly against my abdomen as he fiddles with knobs to get the water going. I want to be offended but maybe it isn't a bad plan considering how much like jelly my legs feel right now. He turns to me and says, "Do you need help undressing?"

Ugh. We are not thinking about what those words out of his mouth are doing to me. Glancing down I realize I am only wearing a large shirt-type nightgown. I have questions about that but they can wait. I kind of need the hand holding me in place. Fuck. "I think maybe I do. I am more than a little concerned that if you release me I am going to melt onto the floor."

He nods, "Put your hands on my shoulders. I will pull

the hem up till I can get a hand on your waist, then you can lift it the rest of the way, if you like."

I nod and try not to think about it as I put my hands on his shoulders. He is quick and gets a hand on my waist sending electricity running through my body from that skin on skin contact. My fingers curl and dig into his shoulders as he pulls the cloth up over my butt, easing it gently between the wall and my body. I take a deep breath and that doesn't help the situation at all, his spicy scent permeates the air. I manage to uncurl my fingers and use one arm to reach down and grab the edge of the shirt. Pulling it slowly over my head and down the other arm to drop it on the floor while he places the other hand on my waist. We both stand there frozen for long moments until he clears his throat, "We should get you in the shower. Yes. In the shower."

He is gentle as he helps me walk into the shower and follows me in, clothes and all. I want to worry about his clothes but honestly, it's probably better this way. I feel weak for all that there is a whole river of desire coursing through my body just begging to be unleashed. The water feels really nice and his hands stay on my waist unmoving while I just let the water run down my body and soak my hair. This all feels amazing. I feel bad that I can't seem to not be entirely turned on by his presence here and he has to suffer through smelling just how he affects me. The heat of the water is relaxing me, but doing absolutely nothing for how weak I feel. "I hate to be the bearer of bad news like this, but I don't have the strength to do more than let the water run over me. I'm so sorry I wasted your time."

He sounds strained as he says, "If you want to be washed and will let me, I will bathe you."

I tip my head back to look up at him, "Are you sure?"

"Yes. I might need you to lean on me for parts of this, but I would do this for you."

"Hum, ok. I don't think this is the best idea but I don't have any others to be honest." He pulls me close to him as he fiddles with bottles and I ask, "How long was I out?"

His hand starts to massage shampoo into my hair as he answers, "Four days inside the building, three since I brought you out of there."

His hand in my hair feels amazing. "That explains why I need to use the facilities so bad right now."

He chuckles, "If you want to pee in the shower, I will pretend I am unaware and never mention it again."

My face may as well be fire the way it feels, "I don't think I have a choice. You promise?"

"I promise. Lay your head back into my hand and close your eyes."

I do as he says, happy to have my eyes closed as my bladder empties. The amount of embarrassment I feel is enormous. I didn't think it was possible to be so relieved and shamed all at the same time in front of a guy that I am also insanely attracted to as he bathes me. This has to be a record. Not that anyone is going to find out to be able to record it. Nope. This secret is dying with me and him.

He tilts my head back up and smooths the water away from my eyes before pulling me closer to lay my head on his chest while he fools with stuff again. It feels like he is smoothing conditioner into my hair, whatever it is, it smells a lot nicer than I did when we started this. He is messing with things behind me again and I tense, realizing what must be next. I am both excited and horrified that he is about to soap up my entire body. I have got to control my reactions. I don't want to make this harder on him than it already is. I feel a cloth, a very thin cloth, covering his hand as he sweeps my hair to one side while he washes my back. His hand, even through the cloth is setting tiny little fires on every nerve ending as he passes over it. My entire being is focused solely on the touch of his hand. He moves across my shoulders and says, "I need to turn you around to wash the front while keeping you supported."

I swallow, oh sweet Goddess he is going to touch the front. My heart rate could keep pace with a dog on the hunt right now, my breathing is pretty ragged and he has only washed my back for crying out loud. "Sure." I help as much as I can, which mostly means that I shuffle my feet around to get myself turned as he guides me and does the actual turning. When I am facing the correct direction his arm tightens around my waist, drawing my body back against his. I can feel his erection pressing against me as he starts moving the cloth across my neck and down my shoulders. Before he is halfway to my breasts I am biting my lip and holding my breath. He circles one breast, making sure to wash every inch of it before repeating the action on the other breast.

It takes all my willpower not to moan.

He continues down my body, slowly and thoroughly, washing every inch of my torso. My breathing grows ever more ragged as he nears my hips and the juncture of my thighs. He lifts the cloth from my body, "I need to lean you against the wall so I can get to your feet."

I nod because nothing I try to say is going to come out coherent right now. He gently pulls me away from him and leans me against the wall of the shower, cool tiles against my back somehow not cooling my overheated skin. I put my hands on the wall to either side of me for balance as he lifts one foot and gently washes it, making sure to get between each toe. I didn't think I was into foot play but I might get there if he keeps playing with my feet. He rinses my foot thoroughly before setting it back down. My breathing is starting to get ragged as he washes the other foot. He finishes it and I hear him opening the bottle for the soap again.

The sweet torment begins with my calves and he works his way up to mid-thigh before moving to the other leg. I am full-on panting at this point, my eyes squeezed shut. When he gets to mid-thigh this time he keeps going on the outside of my leg, before moving to the outside of the other leg. An eternity later, he moves to my inner thighs and works his cloth-covered hand between them. He brushes against my lips and I moan. I can't help it. He works the cloth back and forth, getting in the crease where thighs and pelvis meet. I could die from the pleasure and the torment of it. He doesn't slip the cloth between my lips, though I desperately want him to do just that. No, he presses through my legs and washes my behind. Very thoroughly and I can't help but moan again. He takes the cloth away and I hear more water spraying. I haven't stopped breathing hard yet, and I am not ready to open my eyes and see his cock straining to break free when I can't have it in me, yet. Which is why I am completely unprepared when he lifts my leg and puts it on his shoulder. The spray of water hits between my open lips and my standing leg gives out completely. He catches me as the sprayer clatters to the shower floor, murmuring, "Sorry, I should have warned you."

"I, um, I don't know that it would have done any good. Uh, maybe we should get me out of here before I embarrass myself. More."

He eases me back to a standing position, with one leg still on his shoulder. "I could take care of this for you, if you wanted that."

My eyes fly open and I look down, seeing only the top of his head, his face pointed directly at my open lips. If I would like that indeed. "Um, huh. Well, would you like that? I mean, before I got the impression that you were trying to not go this route with me. I don't think there is any turning back for either of us if we start doing this. Don't get me wrong, I would love to have you kissing my pussy till I scream—" Before I can finish the sentence his mouth is on my lips, his tongue swirling round my clit and flicking it. My leg gives out again as my eyes roll back in my head, his hand catches me and I quickly find myself pressed against the shower wall with both legs resting on his shoulders as he feasts. I hear his zipper open and I feel his shoulder moving under my thigh as he works to suck my soul from my body.

The world explodes into light as I come on his face and he quickly moves from my clit to tongue fucking me. He moans into me as his body tenses and jerks a couple times. His tongue slows and withdraws. My breathing is still pretty ragged but slowing as he slowly takes my legs from his shoulders. He tells me, "I am going to use the spray and my hand to rinse you, ok?"

"Yes, I can probably even stay standing this time."

He rinses me, running his hand between my folds to ensure I am well-rinsed. It causes a few more minor convulsions but I manage to stay upright. I hear his zipper again and then his hands are on my waist as he says, "Let's get you dried off."

Eirene

My office is calm and quiet as I work, tallying the accounts. For all that Conrí swore by babying the peasants, profits are up since his death. Meaning that the expenses from my redecorating and remodels haven't even touched the savings or the investments income. I wonder how annoyed would these lords be if they realized that I own the homes that most of them live in. They think the kings bought them when they were money hungry. But no, the kings never heard about it. Only Conrí's company, Twelve Kings Investments heard about it, and scooped them up, one by one. Now, even if the peasants all die, I'll still have my income.

I am still chuckling over the image of the lords faces were they to find out when my God speaks, "Eirene. You must be there."

"Where must I be, my God?"

"You must be there for the battle. You will learn things that you must know for the final battle."

"This isn't the final? Very well. Is there someone I need to watch in particular?"

"You must go and learn all you can. The final battle will not be decided by this land's people alone. You will need many more in order to defeat the kings. Numbers of the like that you haven't got on this island."

"Will you be sending those numbers?"

"I will. At the right time. Now go. Do as I have instructed."

"As you will, so I do." After long moments spent recovering my heart rate, hearing a voice suddenly in a room I have been alone in for some hours does nothing good for it. "Flavi!"

She enters the room moments after I called for her, "Yes ma'am?"

Grabbing a sheet of paper I tell her, "I need to get this to Lord Ingemar now. Have one of the guards take it to him, make certain it's a guard, the man is disgusting and his wife just died. Tell him to wait for a response."

I dash off a note telling Ingemar,

I have been informed that I must be at the battle to come. I think it would be best if

we arrive together. You may come to my home and we will go in one of my vehicles, my driver is excellent in a pinch, in case something goes awry.
Eirene

Folding the paper I pass it to Flavi, watching as she curtsies and walks fast to the door. She's such a good servant.

Twenty-Four

INGEMAR

That damned woman has decided to arrive with me. I hate it, especially arriving in her vehicle. It makes me look bad in front of the other lords. It doesn't matter that I am king, I still have an image to maintain, especially right now as I am working to take my castle and the actual crown, from the monsters we have let rule us for so long.

As I arrive at her home an idea occurs to me. I exit my vehicle and I see her man, with the vehicle at the ready. Walking over and flashing a note she wrote at him, I say, "I guess she didn't tell you that she wanted you to drive my vehicle instead. Go ahead and put that one away, my man will pass the keys for mine to you. We should arrive with the new royal emblem flying anyway."

The man nods, taking it at face value and puts her vehicle away. I tell my man to let the other drive as I pass by him. He shrugs and pulls the key out of his pocket.

After I knock it is entirely too long a wait before one of

her people answers the door. And it is that damnable Flavi. Walking slowly as ever. Today, I have had enough of this game. I reach forward and grab her arm, spinning her around and crushing her body to mine, "I realize that you and your mistress are playing some cute game, with you taking your time. That game is at an end now, or I will bend you over my knee and spank you till you beg for mercy. Are we clear?" I smack her ass once, just to make sure she fully understands. Her eyes are huge as she nods. "I asked a question and I expect a verbal response."

"Y-yes, sire."

Hm, that's hot. Maybe I will have my women call me sire all the time. "Very good. Let's go."

I release her and she leads me to Eirene's office without any further delays. Knocking on the door she opens it and announces me, I push past her into the room.

Eirene glares at me, "Ingemar, you will not abuse my help. Take your ire out on your own people, not mine. Are we clear?"

"Eirene, I am king now. I think it is well past time you stopped pretending that you are the one in control."

She raises a brow, "Is that so?"

"It is. Now, if you plan to go, come along. My army is assembled and I have no intention of waiting till nightfall to lead them to the castle. It would be quite useful if you could remove the vine wall around the castle."

She smiles at me, "Of course, is there anything else I can help you with?"

"Not at the moment, I will let you know when the crown requires further assistance from you." That ended, I lead the way from the room to the front door, waiting only for one of her people to open it. She enters the sunny day with a wide smile on her face. It is odd, and a little creepy. Her man opens the door and I allow her to climb into the vehicle first, following her close enough to unnerve her.

Instead of being unnerved she seats herself with that same smile on her face. Now, I am nonplussed as the vehicle starts and takes us to the armory.

At the armory we both exit the vehicle, I go first and leave her to follow. The troops are soon cheering to see me. I stop before them to offer encouragement, "My dear people, all of this is for you. We fight so that your families may be safe from the depredations of the monsters that have ruled over us for centuries. We fight for the freedom to govern ourselves. Above all, we fight for an end to tyranny.

It is my hope that the monsters will see our army and know that we are done with them; that we will take no more.

Either way, victory will be ours!"

The men cheer and wave their weapons around like the morons they are. A horse is brought for me and I see Eirene has already mounted hers. "Care to ride next to me as we follow the troops up?"

She is still smiling, it's getting weird. "I would love to converse with you my lord."

"King. I am the king now, Eirene. You would do well to remember that."

"Of course, your highness. How silly of me to forget such an important detail. I am honored to ride with you."

Valdís

It been a full day since the shower and I want him. I won't pressure him, so I have been doing my best to keep myself occupied teaching these twelve women how to access their power. It has kept me occupied today and given me the opportunity to check on my power. It is returned fully.

I need to go home and spend a couple days or a week recovering from whatever they were shooting into my bloodstream. I seem to remember Chance saying something about a scientist, I wonder what happened to him?

The women are practicing small magics here inside the house where no one will be able to see them. They are grasping things fast as they swap stories about the people left behind. Most are orphans, parents murdered or disappeared. Some had a parent on their deathbed when they were kidnapped. And now I wonder, how long have they been kidnapping women from our country and performing tests on them to try and remove their power?

Excusing myself I stand slowly and start for the bathroom. It's like my body has been making up for all the time I was unconscious by making me have to go every twenty minutes. As I come out of the bathroom with a sigh of relief, Chance steps in front of me, "You are avoiding me."

"What? Well, yes. But probably not for the reason you think. And don't step out in front of someone like that. If I wasn't so damned weak right now I would have kicked your nuts clean up to your chin."

"I think you are avoiding me because you want me."

"Well, if you know the reason, then why are you bothered by it? You don't want this to go farther and I don't want to trap you into anything, no matter how grateful I am for the release yesterday in the shower. I'm trying to be a decent person!"

Chance laughs, "You are trying to be a decent person? The woman that went round unknown-to-her-lands rescuing strangers? The woman that knew what was coming and sent everyone away to protect them? You have surpassed decent. Why are you avoiding me?"

Looking down at the tiles beneath my bare toes, I whisper, "Because I don't want to see how much you wish you didn't want me. I don't want to see how much you don't care for me. I don't want to make you uncomfortable because I am there with my scent, making your body respond even though you don't want to."

"I see. You are protecting me from me." He takes my hand and leads me to the bed, pushing me to sit. Kneeling in front of me he looks up at me, "From the moment I saw you I knew you were trouble. I wasn't wrong. You are proving to be the most troublesome, kind, honest, and caring creature I have ever met. I knew the fight was over within moments of you walking into the room my brothers had hauled me off to, about the time all the memories hit. Do you want to know what I remembered?"

"Maybe? Do you want me to know?"

"I do."

"Then yes, if you want me to know."

"I remembered all the time I spent wandering our land looking for you. I remembered the night I was walking the beach and a young girl was tossed screaming off a cliff and into the freezing waters. I remembered diving into the water and rescuing that girl, keeping her safe and warm till morning. I remembered the scent of that girl. How leaving her lying on the beach when her family came hunting her was like ripping off an arm and I didn't understand why because I didn't have the other memories to go with the scent.

Hekate told me before she left that I would find you long before I could know who you were. When I saw you, smelled you that day in the castle, I knew you were the girl I had rescued years ago. My brothers told me you are our queen and I couldn't accept it. I couldn't accept that I could have saved you from what had to have been years more abuse by whoever tried to murder you that night. I was so determined that it couldn't be you that I became certain you were plotting the downfall of us all. Which is how I came to be spying on you the day you left the castle. And why I dove through the portal. Even then I wasn't willing to believe. Until you were taken. Watching you sacrifice your-self and knowing you were counting on me to save you, I couldn't deny the truth any longer. It was my queen they had, and I would do anything to get you back."

"It was you? You were the reason I didn't drown or freeze to death that night?"

"It was me. I almost took you home to the castle right then. Solely because I felt that any child whose family would throw them off a cliff deserved to be a completely spoiled orphan living in a castle. I watched as they collected you. I saw the looks Eirene gave you when she thought no one would see her."

"I thought it was a dream. I thought I had dreamed a whole man rescuing me from the ocean. I made up an entire story about you being held back by a curse and that was why we couldn't be together, unless I found a way to break the curse. Of course, I also thought I was at least partially delusional so I never told anyone. That was the only part of the story I kept for myself, even Malic doesn't know."

He chuckles, "Well, you were close. I was so tired of searching that I gave up and just spent most of my time out in the woods. Not long after I rescued you."

"I'm sorry I disturbed your peace. I can take us all home so you can go do whatever you would rather be doing."

He takes my hands in his, "That is not at all what I want. I have been trying to tell you all this time that I want you, I need you, you are the queen I found so long ago and I want never to let you out of my sight again. I would have you as my queen to jealously guard against all harm. If you would have me."

"Of course I would! How could I not? I have wanted nothing else since the moment I saw you, well, when you didn't have me thinking about hanging you upside down. You were the dark, broody prince of my fantasies." With a chuckle I add, "Back when I thought there would be only one."

He smiles, "I doubt anyone dreams about having twelve

lovers. Or maybe they do. The fantasies of your past aren't the point. Are you certain? I don't want to push you into anything, no matter that I would still shadow you for the rest of your life and definitely kill anyone that so much as looked oddly in your general direction."

"When you put it like that..." I laugh, "I told you, I have dreamt of you since you rescued me. Yes, I would have you. I don't think I am up to the aerobic part of having you yet, but I would very much like to. I think I need to go home and recuperate."

"I agree. How long before you can make a portal to go home?"

"I could probably do it now, but it might be better to wait until after I have eaten."

"Then let's get you fed. I'll feel better to have you at home where we have a lot more security and places to hide you in case things go wrong."

I reach up and pat his cheek, "You're cute, but I'm not hiding ever again."

Knox

Our lookout saw them gathering this morning. Malic and I have never been so grateful that Valdís took off to save people as we are right now. With her out there she is safe from these stupid assholes. Malic is coordinating the armory, dispersing weapons to any that need replacements or simply need them because they aren't usually in the position of possibly having to defend the castle from our own damn people. Cook, he is in the kitchen, cooking up a storm. When I told him that he could have the weapon of his choice from the armory he laughed at me and said, "No offense sire, but I have all the tools I need here to fully butcher a man if that was what I planned for dinner. I think I'll stick with the weapons I know."

I couldn't argue with that so I carried myself off to inform those with less weapons. And made a mental note to not to piss off Cook. We aren't the easiest to kill, but I think being butchered might do it. Not only that, I noticed all the helpers had knives near them too. I think he's been training the helpers and we should maybe make a noise or something before we go wandering in there. I've been through the entire castle. I asked the witches to go down to the safe zone underground. They all just stared at me in silence until I left, so I have no idea if they plan to do as I asked or not. Frankly, I am a little scared to ask considering as Dagma and the two K's were at the front of the group. The two K's have caused more fuckery in this castle, since they got back, than I really know what to do with. The guards are terrified and when they hear cries for help now, they run in the other direction.

I have to get Dagma or Valdís to talk to them when everything calms down. Much of our guard has gathered in the main room, in front of the barred main door. The garage has been closed and lowered into the ground entirely. Hopefully everything below is fine, we never got around to testing it with items inside.

My tasks completed, I head for the main room and I am greeted by the sight of the fifty or so guards we had available to be the main force and all the witches. Fucking hell. The guards slide out of the way as I head for Dagma, who appears to be the damned ringleader here. "What are you all doing here? This is not where I told you to be!"

Dagma raises her brows at me, "I am fully aware of that. I'm sure you are fully aware that we did not agree to do what you said."

"I am. I am entirely aware of that. I am also aware that it will break Valdís's heart if the women she worked so hard to save, that she allowed herself to be captured to save, are murdered in a bloody battle before she can even get back here!"

Dagma moves closer and in a very low voice says, "You should calm down your highness. A nervous king unable to control his emotions just before a battle is bad for morale. We are not without defenses of our own. In fact, some of the women have been strengthening the castle all morning. We have all been practicing offensive magics, and they will help. These women can prevent a lot of death, or dispense it. Do not try to deny them the right to fight. Especially the women that have left homes and children because there is no safety on this big island outside this castle. You cannot prevent them, but you can help keep them safe while they protect you. And they will protect everyone here. We knew this was coming. We have not been idle all this time. And quite honestly, my mother and aunt have been intentionally frightening your guards to keep them out of our business.

Will you work with us or do we fight you and them together?"

I bring a hand up to rub my forehead as I sigh, "Fuck. Ok. Please ask them to stop terrifying the guards, and I will tell them to not interfere while they stand guard to protect you. They aren't as effective frightened like that. As for now, yes. We will work with you. I would prefer that you all move to the second floor. You can split your forces to maintain sight on the interior as well as outside while being above it all. Perhaps you can make it so they can't see inside any of the windows? Is that possible? I would like to utilize your collective powers to the best of their ability while keeping everyone as safe as possible. Will that work for you?"

"Yes, we can certainly work with an inclusive plan." She turns and starts marshaling her charges up the stairs as my phone pings. Pulling it out of my pocket and unlocking it I gasp as I read Chance's message.

I quickly type and send-

> Not today! Wait till we send word, an army is marching on the castle now. Don't let her come here, it isn't safe!

Twenty-Five

Valdís

I can't wait to get home. I miss my kings, I miss my mom and my grandmothers, and I just really miss the smells of home. The places I have been all have an odd scorched smell to them that I really don't like. I am finishing my sandwich when Chance gets a message. A sudden tension sweeps over him and his face shuts down.

So when he looks at me and smiles widely saying, "Why don't we wait to go home? I wouldn't mind having you all to myself for a couple days before we go home where it will be three of us looking to have your attention."

It is absolutely no surprise to me that all of my senses start screaming to go home right this very instant. What is surprising, is how very calm I am as I ask, "What was in the message Chance?"

His smile never slips, "Just Knox saying how he can't

wait to have you home, but he is surprised that I didn't try for more time alone with you."

"Bullshit. I saw your face. Tell me the truth or I will leave you hanging here midair till I close the portal behind me. I fucking hate being lied to Chance, even if you think it's for my own good."

He scrubs a hand over his face, "Fuck. Fine. He said not to come home, an army is marching on the castle right now and he wants you safe. I simply interpreted it creatively in an attempt to stop you from what you are about to do."

Standing I ask him, "What exactly do you think I m going to do, Chance?"

"I think you are going to go home and lay waste to everyone trying to hurt your kings and your family. You will use up too much energy and possibly hurt yourself."

"You are mostly right. I'm not killing anyone. But I am going home. Are you going to fight me on this?"

He sighs, "Will you keep me by your side? I'll support whatever your plan is, as long as you at least keep me beside you for protection."

"Agreed. Come, we haven't any time to waste."

Malic

I've seen this all before, I just didn't think that I would see it in my homeland. From the top of the castle walls I can see them. I remember a time when our people numbered so few that there would not have been enough to fill the ranks of the army marching on our castle. Our land has been prosperous, for all that we wanted little to do with managing it in recent decades.

Our people have multiplied and now number at nearly a hundred thousand. This false king behind the troops, has gathered at least two thousand men and armed them all. It looks like they haven't gotten Outsider weapons yet, only swords. I suppose that is a good thing.

I am still standing here watching, when I smell her. At first I think it must be the scrap of cloth I carry in my pocket, but no. This is fresh. This is her. My heart nearly stops with fear, oh sweet Goddess, what is she doing here now?

Why didn't anyone stop her?

Running through the castle I follow my nose directly to her bedroom.

Valdís

I make sure to send everyone else through first. I have a feeling that if Malic or Knox finds me in front of an open portal, they are going to toss me back through it. Chance waits with me as the twelve women and two former security guards make their way through the portal. Once they are through we step through together, my hand held firmly in his, as though he is worried I'll run.

As soon as we make it through I close the portal. Looking at Chance I ask, "You think they'll be mad?"

He laughs, "I think Malic is going to hug you and hit me. Don't worry, it won't hurt."

I look to the people that came with us, "Well, let's get you introduced to your new home."

They follow us to the door but, before we can touch the knob the door flies open to reveal Malic, "What are you doing here?" He looks at Chance, "You couldn't keep her gone for at least one more day? What the fuck are you good for?"

"Malic," he ignores me to hit Chance. And that is when I decide to coat his body in ice. I leave his neck and head free, he turns his head to glare at me. "If you ignore me now there's a price. I haven't spent my time idle Malic. You know good and well that Chance had no say in whether or not I come home now. Are you going to behave or shall I have Chance push your frozen ass into the hall so we can continue on?"

He rolls his eyes at me, "I won't apologize for wanting you safe. I can say I won't hit Chance again. For this. Let me out, I want a hug."

I set him free with a smile and he snatches me into his arms, hugging me tight. As I wrap my arms around him Knox comes down the hall at a run, skidding to a stop behind Malic. And asking, "Why is she here? My directions were real fucking clear, not today."

Chance laughs, "Go ahead and ask her how she feels about your directions."

"Knox, how did you manage to convince yourself that

he would be the one able to force me not to go somewhere? Come, hug me, and then we need to get these women with the rest of the witches. I know Dagma isn't hiding some where. Where are they?"

He joins in the hug, holding me tightly as he says, "They are on the second floor landing."

Twenty-Six

Valdís

Once I manage to pry the kings off of me, not that I tried too hard at first, I lead the way out of my bedroom to the landing on the second floor. My mom comes running at me and hugs me hard. It is the best feeling ever as I return her hug. She releases me and I tell her, "Chance found some more of us. I trained them a very little bit but they can help if they are paired with someone. Have you got this? Can I leave you to it?"

She snorts, "Of course. Where are you going?"

I smile at her, "To destroy illusions."

She nods, "Be safe. We need you."

Turning toward my kings I tell them, "I am going to walk out that front door and use a whole lot of magic. I am going to use some of it to make sure that I stay upright because while my magic is recovered fully, my body is not. I would really like it if you would support me in this and stand with me, but if you cannot, well, you will stand right here till I finish what I came to do."

Malic looks like he would very much like to explode, instead he says, "Let's walk over here away from the crowd." He pulls me away with Knox following and Chance hangs back briefly, speaking to the two security guards we brought with us before catching up. We step around the corner and Malic pushes me against the wall, "You said you wouldn't do foolish things that would put your life in danger! You promised! Now you want to walk out in front of a couple thousand people that are here to kill us all? This is not you keeping your promise."

I smile at him, "Letting those people catch me was not keeping my promise. For that I can apologize, but I had no choice in the matter. It had to happen. This is not that. I am here, telling you what I am going to do. Giving you the opportunity to come with me and be my protector. I am not letting people die if there is a way for me to prevent it. And I can. Hekate taught me some things while I was in that drugged up haze. They weren't entirely clear until Knox told Chance to keep me from coming home today. Now, those lessons are crystal clear. I know how to live through this. How to protect the people inside this castle and the ones outside it as well." I bring my hands up, placing one on each side of his face, "This has to happen. Come with me and you can all three ensure that nothing gets me while I do magic tricks for our people."

He brings his forehead down to touch mine, "I thought I would lose my mind when you were kidnapped by the organization. I was told that I was not allowed to go get you. Waiting was an eternity and now you are here. I just want to wrap you in blankets and put you in the safe room. But no, you need to go save people. Our people, who are being manipulated by the Outsiders once again and I can't help but think that maybe we should let them have this place. We need you. Not this land. Just you. If you die, we are all of us lost."

"I know, my Malic, I know. I can tell you for sure, that I am not dying today. But we need to go do this. I can feel them drawing closer. We need to go before the battle is engaged. Before I run out of steam physically."

"All right. All right. Let's go do this. But then we are locking you in your bedroom until you are fully recovered."

"Malic, is this really the time to talk dirty to me?"

Knox and Chance laugh loudly as Malic steps back and offers his arm to escort me to the doors of the castle. Chance and Knox follow us, Chance asking, "How come you never threaten to hang him in mid air?"

Knox laughs, "Maybe it's because Malic wouldn't be as entertained by that sort of thing as you would."

"I would find it wholly entertaining to be hung upside down for a brief period of time."

Malic turns his head and murmurs, "I will not find that amusing. At all. Please do not do that to me."

"I won't. This isn't really the greatest time to discuss it but since I am walking so slow anyway, why not. You remember hearing about how my stepmother had me thrown off a cliff?" He nods, his lips pressing into a thin line, "Well, as it turns out, someone did save me. I just thought it was my imagination."

"What? Who?"

"Chance. That was one of the things he remembered after I said her name to him. He saved me and kept me warm the whole night."

"Well damn. I guess all that time he spent searching for you did pay off. I owe him a lot of money." Standing before the doors he asks, "How do you want to do this?"

"I want the three of you to go out before me and I am going to raise a small portion of the earth so that we can get up high enough for my voice to carry. Once we are up there, the three of you stand behind me. Ok?"

"Very well." He nods to the guards flanking the door and they pull the huge bar out of the holder, it swings silently back to its home against the wall. Two guards move to the handles and pull them, swinging the doors in and allowing us to view the sea of people standing before the castle.

Fuck, that's a lot of people. Deep breath, I can do this. My kings walk out before me, stopping a few yards out from the castle. I follow slowly. These people need to realize who orchestrated this. I feel all the eyes on me as I walk out and stop well away from the kings.

Pulling my magic around me, I raise a small section of earth, making a platform at the top large enough for all of us and stairs leading up to it from the part facing us. Fuck, I don't know if I can make it up those stairs. This sucks. All right, what if I wrap the magic around myself and float the fuck up there? My body is still weak but the magic is on point.

I hear Chance snicker as I float past them, still upright

but definitely not walking. The three of them are directly behind me on the stairs and I know as I set myself down that if I were to stumble, they would not let me fall. Thankfully, my legs stay steady beneath me.

Aside from some knocking of my knees. This is really a lot of people. And look, there in the back are my stepmother and Lord Ingemar. Good.

Quickly reciting the spell Hekate taught me to make my voice carry, I begin my little speech.

"I know you all have come here to make war upon the kings of our land and that my name has been used as a rallying point. I want to tell the truth about what has brought you here."

Lord Ingemar shouts, "She is nothing more than a pawn of the kings, don't listen to her!"

Lifting my hand I send a very visible bit of magic at him that silences him. The silence is temporary but, effective. I try not to laugh as his face gets red from trying to shout and making no sound at all. "My name is Valdís. I am the one they said was kidnapped from her home. Nothing could be further from the truth. In truth I ran away from certain death at the hands of the woman that claims to be my mother. That woman is Eirene Potentus, and she is no kin to me at all, as she is one of the Outsiders! I have seen the mark on her ear, and on the ear of the woman I always thought my sister. I am the sole surviving heir of Conrí Potentus, born from his union with Dagma Vitamata.

Lord Ingemar is at best, a schemer and liar. When I sought help from him to end my stepmother's tyranny, he imprisoned me and attempted to force me to marry his son.

At worst, he is a traitor to our lands, working with an Outsider to overthrow our kings."

Eirene shouts, "Lies! The child has ever been confused and ill. That is why our courts granted me the inheritance. I want nothing more than to care for my poor, mentally unstable daughter."

"Show them your ear then. Let them see the mark!" I smile now, as the color drains from her face when all these people look to her. "My people, I have a gift for you. Our deity has long kept her name hidden in the mists. Kept her presence from us. Her time of hiding is at an end. She is back and her name is **Hekate!**"

The people before me and probably quite a few behind me, fall to the ground stunned. The only ones that don't are the outsiders. "Eirene, you tell your god he is finished in this land. The witches are back and we are not playing nice any longer."

A male voice projects from Eirene's throat, "You would defy me little witch?"

Hekate whispers in my ear, "You definitely would. Taunt him. He cannot hurt you or anyone here."

"I absolutely defy you, go back to your own lands and leave our people in peace!"

The voice laughs and Eirene's hand comes up, sending a wave of power at the crowd. The only ones affected are the ones that didn't fall after the mention of Hekate's name. The Outsiders. Every one of them falls to the ground, eyes open and unseeing. Eirene's face is comical as her jaw drops.

"It would appear that didn't work out quite the way

you expected. Take yourself away from here, you and your people will never again hold power in these lands."

I turn to start for the stairs when Malic's face changes and he shoves me into Knox. When I turn it is just in time to see him throw an arrow back at Eirene. It lands in the dirt next to her horse. She smiles and turns the horse away, riding slowly back toward her home.

Chance says, "Malic, your aim is shit."

He shrugs, "I haven't thrown an arrow in over five hundred years. It still landed next to her, I think that isn't bad."

I laugh and look at all those bloody steps. I can't do that. Wrapping magic around all of us for stability I lower the platform back into the earth and then release the magic holding us in place. Dagma greets me at the door, "I am so proud of you. Now go to bed. We'll have food sent up for all of you. Cook is likely to bring it himself to be sure you are safe. After he tastes it to be sure it is safe for you."

"It will be good to see him."

I start to say more but am cut off as Knox lifts me into his arms, "Sorry Dagma, she needs to go rest. Keep the guards with you while you check the army, they'll know what to do with the bodies of the Outsiders. Make sure your witches all see the mark, so they know what to watch for, we haven't seen the last of them."

With that I am whisked away to my bedroom, to rest and cuddle with my kings.

～

It's been three days since I revealed her name to everyone. The men that were floored by hearing it all got up an hour or so after I was taken to my room. They have since joined the guard and trainings are being held all over the mountain now. Some of them were never found. Like the lords that were the leaders of the movement. We sent soldiers to my home, to take it from Eirene. It was empty of all people. I plan to go there very soon and collect my father's diary.

My brother has revealed that he also joined the guard and I am as happy for him as I am worried.

I am training with the witches, we have taken over one of the other castles for it. I have continued my mission to bring our witches home, some are bringing entire families. The difference is that now I simply open the portal to where they will be, instead of traveling around in the Outsiders lands. At first we were concerned about the food supplies, but then the offerings started appearing at the doors to the castle. Every night, the farmers, most who have sons now in the guard, bring food and leave it at the door. We have had to station guards there in shifts to keep the food from attracting various wild animals. The guards always thank them for even the tiniest bit, one guard even happened to be on duty when his father came to leave his offering.

The people have realized that they were manipulated, at least the ones that bought into what those lords were doing. The women that left their homes for the shelter of the castle have checked their homes to see if it is safe to return. Some took guards with them and brought the rest of their things back with them. One found that her husband had moved another woman in, she wished the woman well as she collected her own things, including her mother's necklace from around the woman's neck.

The ones that cannot return to their homes have now permanently moved into the castle we practice at, and we all practice our defensive spells by layering them upon the castle.

My kings are my constant companions. One is always with me. Whoever can be spared from the work of running the kingdom, which seems to be mostly back to normal, is with me. The vendors from the food market are upset that it hasn't been reopened. They became more upset when they were told that the farmers would be selling their own wares from now on as the vendors were not to be trusted. They vowed that the tyranny of these kings would be overthrown and immediately fell to the floor screaming as the word traitor branded itself across their necks. That certainly had nothing to do with the fire witch I asked to sit in the throne room to work on her embroidery, she was far too engrossed in her work.

Hekate is here at the castle we practice in today. She hugged Chance and told him that he did very well. Then she turned to me and said, "A storm is coming. The Outsiders and their God have not given up. We will talk more in your dreams, but you must all prepare."

"It will be done."

She took herself off then to go greet every one of the now nearly one hundred witches in residence at the castle.

Chance tells me that Gage will be here within the next two days and he is mad as hell about the whole thing.

I can't wait to see how he is going to react to my presence or that of my witches, as Chance also told me that he hasn't been told about everything that happened here.

Surely he won't be as irritating as Chance was, right?

~Author's note ~

Hi! I hope you have enjoyed this book as much as I enjoyed writing it. If you liked this, I have a free novella for anyone that signs up for my newsletter. I don't email more than once a month and I hate spam too. Sign up link - https://www.subscribepage.com/r4v6m2

If you loved this book, a review is super helpful and extra appreciated.

Thank you for reading what the voices in my head talk about while I should be sleeping.

Rhiannon

About the Author

Rhiannon writes steamy paranormal romance. She is an avid reader of many authors in a variety of genre though she tends more toward paranormal.

She has three former pound puppies that she dotes on and three daughters that she adores.

Rhiannon has lived in multiple states though she is currently residing in North Carolina. Wandering, witching, and reading with her puppies and husband are what she does when she isn't writing.

To learn about what is happening in Rhiannon's world and get loads of pupper cuteness, sign up for the newsletter by using the QR code below to visit my website.

Also by Rhiannon Futch

The Daughter of the Moon series-

Selena Rose, Daughter of the Moon Book 1

Thorns of the Rose, Daughter of the Moon Book 2

Heart of the Rose, Daughter of the Moon Book 3

The Fate's Chronicles series

A Vampire's Fate

A Vampire's Treasure

A Vampire's Dream

A Vampire's Chase

A Vampire's Fight

Fated for Halloween - only available via email signup

The Belancore Witches of North Carolina series

Witchy Ever After

A Witchy New Year

My Witchy Valentine

Sin series

Sin on a Dark Knight

Sin on a Broken Heart

Sin on a Burning Heart

Sin on a Vengeful Heart

The Vampire Kings Series

Mercy of the Vampire King

Shame of the Vampire King

Pursuit of the Vampire King

Prey of the Vampire King

Reign of the Vampire King

Coming Soon

Love and Vampires Series

Olivia's Fall

Olivia's Prison

Olivia's Flight

Olivia's Family

Warriors of the Old Gods

A Dream of Blood

A Dream of Wolves

A Dream of Stone

A Dream of Ravens

A Dream of Bones